"So, we're agreed to ignore your grandfather's idea that I'm the woman you should marry, right?" Brittnie said briskly.

"And in future, we'll treat each other with only professional courtesy," she continued.

"If we can manage that," Jared agreed.

"Fine." She turned to go before she did something crazy like telling Jared that she couldn't think of him in a businesslike way, when she found him so compelling, intriguing and downright sexy.

But Jared was blocking her way. "After all, it's not as though we're attracted to each other…. And just to prove it we should try an experiment."

Before she had time to respond, that quirky smile of his met her lips. The world spun, righted itself, and then spun in the opposite direction.

At last he pulled away, as breathless as she was. "What do you think?" Jared nuzzled her cheek with his nose. "Can we treat each other in a professional way?"

Dear Reader,

I've always been fascinated by strong women, which is one of the reasons I love romance novels. MARRIAGE TIES is a series about a family of such women: a mother, her stepdaughter and two daughters. To test their strength, I teamed them up with men who are anything but tame. The Kelleher women are strong, though they don't always know how their strength will be tested. But then, none of us knows until it happens.

I hope you enjoyed the first book in this series, *Another Chance for Daddy*, and are ready for *Wedding Bells*. In this book, Brittnie Kelleher is hired by businessman Jared Cruz for her dream job. But there are a couple of snags to her happiness. Not only does she find herself responsible for looking after his stubborn grandfather, but she also falls for Jared himself—even though he insists his interest in her is purely professional!

Next year, look out for Shannon Kelleher's story. She meets a *Bachelor Cowboy* who thinks he has very good reasons for staying that way. Then, late in 1999, look for *Resolution: Marriage*, the story of Mary Jane Kelleher, the mother to these three women, who is reunited with her high-school sweetheart and must come to terms with a secret that she's kept for more than twenty-five years.

Be prepared to laugh and maybe to cry, but certainly to enjoy the strength and resourcefulness of Rebecca, Brittnie, Shannon and Mary Jane.

Happy reading,

Patricia Knoll

Wedding Bells
Patricia Knoll

Marriage
Ties

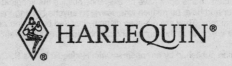

HARLEQUIN®

TORONTO • NEW YORK • LONDON
AMSTERDAM • PARIS • SYDNEY • HAMBURG
STOCKHOLM • ATHENS • TOKYO • MILAN • MADRID
PRAGUE • WARSAW • BUDAPEST • AUCKLAND

ISBN 0-373-03530-6

WEDDING BELLS

First North American Publication 1998.

Copyright © 1998 by Patricia Knoll.

This edition published by arrangement with Harlequin Books S.A.

® and TM are trademarks of the publisher. Trademarks indicated with ® are registered in the United States Patent and Trademark Office, the Canadian Trade Marks Office and in other countries.

Printed in U.S.A.

CHAPTER ONE

As SHE saw it, Brittnie Kelleher had two options. Either she could ignore Steve Wilberson or she could be rude to him.

She had already tried hiding from him, which had done nothing except make her look foolish. In fact, she had spent the past five minutes looking foolish. Brittnie glanced up from her crouching position behind a display of Native American pottery and smiled wanly at the salesclerk who was leaning over the top of the glass case, viewing her with a puzzled look.

Brittnie cleared her throat. "Lovely things," she said in a bright tone. She pointed to a squat pitcher with a handle shaped like an elongated eagle's head. "That one is especially beautiful."

"Uh, yes. Yes, it is," the confused lady responded. "We have several pieces by that artist. He's very talented."

Brittnie nodded as if her head was attached to a spring. "Oh, yes, I can see that."

"Would you like for me to take it out of the case so you...?"

"Oh, thank you, but no," Brittnie chirped. "I can see it fine from right here."

"No kidding." The salesclerk sniffed. She took out a cloth and began polishing the glass.

Brittnie gave her an apologetic little shrug, but she didn't move away like any sane person would have.

Instead, when the saleslady turned around, Brittnie raised herself enough to peek out the window.

Darn. Steve was still outside. His red hair and ruddy complexion drew attention even as the scowl on his too handsome face made passersby do a double take, then skirt around him warily.

Brittnie dropped back to rest on her heels and pressed her lips together in irritation. She cursed the luck that had brought her into his line of sight today. He'd started after her like a bloodhound on the scent. He knew she'd slipped into one of the little shops that lined Durango's Bartlett Avenue, but he didn't know which one. He was smart enough not to search by cruising in and out of the shops, knowing that she might emerge from one while he was inside another. Instead, he dawdled in the middle of the sidewalk, his gaze roaming the area like a spy waiting for a contact to deliver a briefcase full of state secrets—or like a police officer searching for a criminal.

No doubt, in his mind, Brittnie *was* a criminal. She'd committed the crime of repeatedly refusing his advances. When this had all started two weeks ago, she'd thought he was joking. After all, his wife Lauren was one of her friends. In fact, Lauren was lifelong friends with Brittnie's sister Rebecca. Brittnie had known Steve for years and had always thought him a nice enough person, but recently he'd begun treating her with far too much familiarity.

Brittnie had been stunned by his pursuit of her, thinking it was a joke, but it hadn't taken her long to understand that he was serious. Once she had realized his true intent, she had avoided any situation where they might be alone, or even in a small group. She never returned his phone calls and now screened her calls on her answering machine before picking up the receiver. Her family had begun to comment on her strange behavior, but she didn't know what else to do. She had told him to leave her alone, but the big idiot had somehow gotten it into his head that she was being coy or playing hard to get.

Brittnie hadn't bothered threatening to tell his wife because he knew her well enough to know she wouldn't hurt Lauren, a sweet, generous woman, by telling her what a lecherous creep she'd married—although since they'd been married seven years, poor Lauren might have already learned that fact. Brittnie also had the option of telling her brother-in-law, Clay, and asking *him* to deal with Steve, but Clay had enough to handle right now. He and Becca were starting their own business and Clay was trying to carve out time to coach his son's soccer team. Brittnie hated to burden him any further. Besides, she couldn't constantly depend on her family to take care of things for her. She was a professional now. She had a reputation to build, and even in personal matters, she had to stand on her own.

So why was she skulking behind a display case? she asked herself ruefully. But she knew the answer to that one. She had an appointment today that could very well determine her future. The last thing she needed was an upsetting confrontation with Steve Wilberson. She knew she would have to deal with it soon, but not today.

Brittnie watched carefully, waiting for her chance. When his back was turned to her, she stood and fled to a corner where Mexican serapes hung alongside T-shirts and fringed leather jackets. She tried to make herself inconspicuous as she pretended to examine a buckskin jacket while darting glances out the window, but she

knew being inconspicuous was impossible. She wasn't
dressed like the tourists in the shop who were spending
this beautiful autumn afternoon shopping for souvenirs.
She wore a navy blue suit in honor of her meeting. True,
the suit wasn't hers. She'd borrowed it from Becca because it made her feel confident when she wore it, even
though her height meant the skirt hit her a few inches
above the knee. The short jacket had a narrow band of
lace around the hem that saved it from looking too severe and businesslike. If she soiled this suit by lurking
around in shops trying to avoid Steve, her sister would
be irked with her.

Besides, she knew she had to get out of here because
her meeting was in—she glanced at her watch and her
eyes widened. Fifteen minutes! She couldn't waste any
more time. She had to get out as discreetly as possible,
but her five-foot-ten-inch frame and bright blond hair
made her about as inconspicuous as a giraffe at a pot-
bellied pig convention.

Now, she realized that she should have hurried into
the Harper Building as soon as she'd parked her car, but,
oh, no, a new bookstore had caught her eye and since
she was early for her appointment, she'd simply *had* to
inspect it. That's when Steve had seen her. She should
have spoken to him right away, but been cool and dis-
tant.

Brittnie grimaced. She already knew exactly what
would have happened if she had spoken to Steve. He
would have flirted with her, embarrassed her, proposi-
tioned her.

She peered out again and saw that he was moving out
of sight. This might be her chance. With a nod to the
saleslady, who looked as though she would be glad to

see the last of her, Brittnie moved to the door, then scurried out when she saw that Steve was looking in the other direction.

She glanced over her shoulder as she made a dash for the office building a few blocks away. Her appointment was on the fourth floor and if she hurried, she could dart inside the elevator before Steve caught up with her. With any luck, he'd go away while she was meeting with Jared Cruz.

"Brittnie! Hey, wait up," Steve called. She could hear his footsteps hurrying after her.

She sighed inwardly and gave a hopeless shake of her head. The truth was that luck hadn't been running in her direction lately, but Steve certainly had.

Acting as though she hadn't heard him, Brittnie pushed through the old-fashioned frosted glass doors and loped across the pink marble floor of the lobby. When the elevator door opened and several people stepped out, she called, "Hold the elevator, please."

A tall, dark-haired man in an elegant gray suit stepped in ahead of her, reached for the Door Open button when she called out, and gave her a sharp glance as she whirled inside.

"Thanks," she gasped, trying to duck into the corner and yet peer around the man's shoulder at the same time. "Fourth floor, please."

From the corner of her eye, Brittnie saw him give her another quick look as he indicated that the button for that floor had already been punched. Brittnie nodded, then pressing herself against the wall, she stared at the doors, willing them to close.

She thought she was going to make her escape, but a man carrying a file box called out for the elevator, too.

Someone hurried up to speak to him and he turned away; but this caused enough of a delay that Steve had time to dash inside the compartment while the gray-suited man held the door.

Brittnie gave the man a disgruntled look, though he certainly couldn't have known that she was trying to avoid Steve. She could feel his gaze rest on her curiously, but she kept her own fixed on the elevator doors.

"Hey, Brittnie," Steve said, smoothing back his hair and straightening his tie. "Didn't you hear me calling you?" He gave her a wide, toothy smile, but his eyes roamed over her statuesque frame in a way that made her think of an old cartoon of the Big Bad Wolf licking his chops as he examined Little Red Riding Hood.

"No, Steve," she said coolly, hating him for putting her in this embarrassing position. "I didn't hear you." On purpose, her tone added as she glanced over her shoulder. Her face was stiff with fury and her eyes were as dark as tornado-breeding clouds.

He gave her an affable smile and opened his hands expansively. "Well, that's okay. No harm done."

That's what he thought, she fumed. She turned her back on him and stared at the lighted panel.

"Thought you might like to have some lunch," he continued.

"No, thank you." Icicles virtually dripped from her tongue. Was the man stupid? she thought furiously. In how many ways did she have to tell him to leave her alone before he got the message?

"Ah, come on, you have to eat," he wheedled.

Brittnie turned her head and gaped at him. She couldn't believe he was pursuing her like this before a stranger, but she didn't know why she was surprised. In the past couple of weeks, everything Steve had done had surprised her—and sickened her.

"Will your wife be joining us?" she asked pointedly as she gave him a cold stare. Behind her, she felt a change in the atmosphere as if the other occupant of the compartment had taken an interest in their conversation.

The car stopped on the second floor, but no one got on. During the delay, Brittnie turned to glance at the other man.

At first, she'd only noticed his suit and his politeness in holding the door for her. Now she saw that he had thick hair that looked black in the muted lighting and intelligent eyes of deep chocolate brown. He seemed to be watching her with interest, noting the fury and frustration that Steve seemed not to notice.

Brittnie was taken aback by his close scrutiny. Ordinarily, she would have turned away, but she was as interested in him as he was in her. She saw that his nose was straight, and his cheekbones were high. In fact, his whole face would have had a certain sharpness if not for the surprising thickness of his eyelashes and his eyebrows which curved enough to soften his features. There was something about his face, which was striking rather than handsome that made her think fleetingly of symmetry and balance, though she didn't know why.

As she glanced at him, his eyebrows lifted ever so slightly as if he was waiting to hear her reply to Steve. For no reason, heat flared in her cheeks.

"Uh, no," Steve said after an awkward pause. "Lauren had to go over to Cortez today. Took the kids to see their grandparents."

So with his wife out of the way, Steve had decided it was time to play. Irritated at him and at the luck that had somehow thrown her in his path today, Brittnie turned to face the front of the elevator, wishing this interminable ride was over. Was this the slowest elevator in the world, or what? She wanted desperately to get to where she was going and leave him behind, but what if he pursued her straight to the office where she had an appointment? Surely he wouldn't be that stupid.

"So will you take pity on a temporary bachelor?"

On the other hand, maybe he would.

Brittnie's eyes fixed on the lighted button for the fourth floor and inspiration struck. There was a way, though not a very honest one, to get out of this, maybe permanently. She lifted her chin and squared her shoulders. "Sorry, Steve. I'm on my way to have lunch with the man in my life."

He stiffened and his face grew surly. "The man in your life? What do you mean?"

She gave him a hard look. "I don't know how to make it any more clear than that, Steve."

"What man?" he blustered. "Lauren said you don't have a boyfriend."

Good grief! He had discussed her with Lauren. Brittnie was horrified enough to answer recklessly, "Jared Cruz. He's expecting me any minute." That part was true, at least. His secretary had called her that morning to confirm their appointment, though it certainly wasn't supposed to include lunch.

Steve stepped close. "Jared Cruz? Of Cruz and Company? The property managers."

"The very same." Brittnie lifted her chin and dared her nemesis to call her a liar.

"When did he become the man in your life?" Steve demanded.

"It's...it's a recent development."

"More recent than you know." The flat statement was spoken in a low, cultured voice by the man standing behind Brittnie. As he said it, he stepped forward, gave Brittnie a direct glance that simmered with curiosity. He held out his right hand to Steve even as he placed his left at the back of Brittnie's waist, causing her to jump. It took her only a second to realize his touch was firm rather than familiar. Her eyes shot up to meet his and he gave her that same cool look.

Her mouth went dry and her heart plummeted with a sick thud. Of course, she thought with helpless resignation as she looked into his eyes. Her luck was running true to form. The one person she most needed to impress favorably was the one who'd caught her in a big, fat lie—about him. What had possessed her to blow such a wonderful opportunity as her appointment with him had promised?

She was trying to form words to stammer out an apology and beg for another chance when he astounded her by saying. "How do you do? Steve, is it? I'm Jared Cruz." He nodded to the other man and propelled Brittnie forward. "And this is our floor. Sorry we don't have time to stop for a chat."

"Hey, hey wait a minute," Steve sputtered as his hand shot out to stop the closing door. "You two acted like you didn't even know each other in here."

"It's a little game we play," Jared answered. He reached back inside, removed Steve's hands from the doors, and punched the button for the ground floor of the building. His polite facade dropped away and he gave Steve a look that would have buckled steel. His voice leveled into a harder tone. "I like to keep an eye out in case she's being followed by a lecherous bastard trying to cheat on his wife. Can't be too careful these days.''

Steve's hand sprang back as if he'd been seared by an electric spark and the elevator doors started to close. His mouth opened and he made a few garbled sounds. It seemed he'd swallowed his own tongue. Good, Brittnie thought. Maybe he would choke on it.

When the soft whoosh of the departing elevator had died away, Brittnie whirled around and looked at Jared Cruz, her gray eyes full of astonishment and dawning gratitude. His glance swept over her, from her hair in its neatly swirled French twist, to her navy blue pumps. Finally, he looked at her face, his expression a mixture of curiosity and disapproval.

In her wildest imaginings, she couldn't think of a more inauspicious beginning to a professional relationship. She cleared her throat. ''Thank you for what you did,'' she said in a tone brimming with awe and nearly breathless with shock.

''I'm not in the habit of lying for a potential employee, Miss Kelleher.'' He looked her over once again. ''You are Brittnie Kelleher, aren't you?''

''Yes, yes, I am.'' Brittnie said, then shrugged, causing her clutch handbag to slip from beneath her arm. She pulled it back into position. Her face was very earnest as she said, ''And I can see where lying for a stranger probably isn't a very good habit to cultivate. I mean, after all, your property management firm has an excellent reputation and much of that is based on your own honesty. You have people all over the state, the world, depending on you to take care of things for them. Truthfulness and integrity mean everything in a business like yours. You certainly wouldn't want to jeopardize that by...." She was babbling in her nervousness. Oh, why didn't she just shut up? She couldn't, though. The words just continued rolling out. "By having people think you're a liar."

Jared had listened to her crazy little monologue with the fascinated expression of a man watching a circus performer on the brink of diving from a fifty-foot-high platform into a puddle of water. Now he inclined his head as he stared at her. "Right. You're welcome. Are you finished now?"

"Yes," she answered in a small voice. Her handbag slipped again and this time Jared caught it one-handed behind her back. He slapped it into her palm and she clasped it with a death grip.

"I admit," he said, looking at her as if her mind was unhinged. "Having people think I'm a liar has never been one of my ambitions."

Brittnie rolled her eyes helplessly. "Of course not. I'd apologize again," she sighed. "But it's beginning to sound redundant." She cleared her throat and gave him a weak smile.

He considered her silently for a moment. "If I decide to hire you, can I assume there'll be no more potential boyfriends following you to work?"

Her mouth dropped open as hope surged upward. "You mean there's still a chance you might hire me?"

"A remote one," he admitted dryly. "Now, about those boyfriends. You'll have no more of them following you?"

Brittnie winced. "Good heavens, I hope not!" She paused, then decided to set him straight on one point at least. "And believe me, Steve Wilberson wasn't a boy-friend, potential or in any other capacity."

"Wilberson," he said softly, his deep, intelligent eyes sharpening as if he was filing the name away for future reference. Then he focused on her and said, "Good. As I recall, we have an appointment. Let's go into my of-fice." He stepped back and gestured toward a nearby door.

Brittnie caught a glimpse of a tasteful brass plaque engraved with the name of his firm. Before they reached the door, it swung open and a man walked out. Brittnie noticed only the dark brown uniform of a parcel delivery service until he stopped directly in her path. Her eyes flew to focus on his face.

"Brittnie?" he asked.

"Oh, Phil, hi," she said, recognizing Phil Stevens, a friend from her hometown, Tarrant.

He looked her over. "Nice suit," he said, his teasing smile widening to a huge grin.

Fully aware of the man who had stopped beside her and was watching her expectantly, Brittnie tried to fight down the embarrassment that burned in her cheeks. "Thank you, Phil," she said tightly.

With a laugh and a wave, he stepped around them and headed for the elevator.

"Another boyfriend?" Jared asked.

"Not since fifth grade," she answered, barely rescu-ing her tone of voice from sounding snappish.

Thankfully, Jared didn't comment, but she desperately wished she knew what he was thinking. She slid a quick glance at his face, which told her nothing. Ever the op-timist, she concluded that things had to get better.

With a hopeful sigh, she stepped to the door where

she again noticed the brass plaque. Somehow the plaque seemed to match its owner. Understated, tasteful, and there was that word again—elegant.

Brittnie had no doubt that the way Jared Cruz presented himself to the world was a true reflection of the way he really was.

She, on the other hand, was a fraud. Phil had seen it, as would anyone who knew her. She liked this suit of Becca's, but it wasn't her style. In reality, she liked snug jeans and loose T-shirts, short skirts, denim vests, dangling earrings and sandals. Her clothing choices stemmed partly from personality and partly from a desire to look like anything except the stereotype of her profession. She knew that the elderly librarian with sensible shoes and a fierce expression which she wore as she quieted disruptive library patrons was someone who hadn't existed for years—if she had ever existed. Nevertheless, the myth persisted and Brittnie liked to do her part to dispel it. Though not today, she thought with another glance at Jared Cruz. This job was too important to her and she'd already made enough of a hash of this interview—which hadn't even started yet.

Jared led her into a reception area that was decorated in muted grays, blues, and burgundies. He spoke to a young woman at a reception desk, picked up a handful of pink message slips, then gestured for Brittnie to precede him down a hallway. As they walked, Brittnie caught sight of his employees in their offices, talking on the phone or working at computer terminals. When they saw him, they nodded or smiled. Brittnie thought it was interesting that his employees didn't have to appear busy when the boss walked by. They *were* busy. Three different people stopped him as they passed, saying they needed to speak to him that afternoon. He said he'd make time, but he never broke his stride. Brittnie wondered how many meetings he scheduled in an afternoon and what time he managed to get away from the office.

Cruz and Company managed real estate all over the area, from office buildings to vacation condominiums. They had a reputation for their responsiveness to their clients' needs. Property owners and renters could expect Cruz and Company to take care of a problem right away whether it was a clogged bathroom drain, or a cracked foundation. That kind of reputation came from hard work, and it seemed that no one worked harder than the boss.

She had found out all she could about the firm before coming for her interview. Her nosiness was due to her unquenchable interest in people and her particular fascination with this man. True to her profession, she had searched out every bit of information she could discover about him. Jared wasn't far past thirty, unmarried, but had been running the family business for a year, since the retirement of his grandfather, Roberto, and had seen an increase in the number of properties his firm managed. He was known for his hard work and dedication—and lack of a personal life.

From what she had learned, Brittnie had concluded that if he wasn't already a full-fledged workaholic, Jared Cruz soon would be—though, of course, it was none of her business, she reminded herself as he opened the door to his own office. He held it as she walked inside.

"Utilitarian" was the word that sprang to her mind as she surveyed the room. The walls held neat bookshelves full of books and photographic prints of Southwestern scenes, but were unadorned with any personal effects. There were no family photographs on the glass-topped mahogany desk, only a state-of-the-art computer, neat stacks of file folders, some writing pads and a precise row of pens and pencils. The room bespoke the owner's businesslike attitude.

Brittnie noticed another door leading out of the office and decided it must be Jared's private washroom. The door was open a crack and she could see a dark blue tile floor through the opening. A nice perk, she thought, to have a private washroom. No doubt, it was one of the benefits of being the owner of the company.

Brittnie was fascinated with Jared's office, but didn't have much time to consider what she had seen because Jared gestured for her to sit in the chair opposite his desk. He walked around his desk to sit in his own chair, but came up short when he bumped into an open file drawer at the front.

"Oomph," he grunted when his shin connected with the drawer.

"Are you all right?" Brittnie asked, starting from her chair.

He waved her back. "Yes, yes. Sit down," he said sharply, then gave the drawer a hard look as if he was trying to understand how it had come to be left open. Finally, Jared sat in his chair and leaned forward. Brittnie couldn't see his hands so she wondered if he was surreptitiously rubbing his shin. After a moment, he straightened and she snapped to attention.

He folded his hands, with fingers interlaced, on his desk blotter and said, "Now, Miss Kelleher, tell me why I should hire you, a woman with less than a year of experience, to sort and organize my great-uncle's things?"

So, Brittnie thought. He had done some research, too, and he believed in getting right to the point.

She took a breath, and plunged in. "It's true that I don't have much experience, but you won't find anyone who's more interested in the subject. I've been fascinated by Colorado history since I first learned to read."

"Fascination doesn't always translate into expertise," he pointed out.

"True, but it almost always insures conscientiousness."

"That depends on the person."

"I'm the person," she answered coolly.

Jared sat back, rested his hands loosely on the arms of his chair, and regarded her with a glint of humor in his eyes. "You're very sure of yourself."

If only he knew. She wasn't nearly as certain as she sounded, and the nervous fluttering in her stomach was proof of that, but she wanted this job so badly it was becoming an obsession. "In this case, I am."

She leaned forward and her eyes shone as she spoke earnestly. She tucked back a strand of hair that had slipped down to tickle her cheek. "Just think what we can learn from the lives of ordinary people like your great-grandparents. They came here at the turn of the century, a young couple barely out of their teens, but willing to homestead, to work hard and prove up on land no one else wanted. They were from Mexico and to make things even harder, they had to deal with prejudice and a new language. Isn't that right?"

The sharpness in Jared's eyes had softened. His attention seemed to be caught by the excitement in her face and the color that was climbing her cheeks. "That's right. My grandfather tells me that they spoke only Spanish.''

"From what I've learned, your great-grandmother, Magdalena, was descended from one of the great houses of Spain. She was an educated woman who taught herself to read and write English, then used her new language to write down everything that happened to her and her husband. There must have been times when she could barely afford the paper to write her journals, but she always found a way because she wanted to leave behind a record for her sons.''

"That's true,'' Jared conceded. "And the journals have been boxed up for fifty years.''

Brittnie lifted her hands triumphantly. "There you go, then. I can take those journals and transcribe the information. It would be a fascinating picture of life here nearly a century ago. And I understand your great-uncle David had many other interesting papers from his law practice that should be preserved. I promise you I will be very careful.''

Jared opened his mouth, made a soft sound of humor, and shook his head. "That won't be as easy as it sounds.''

Brittnie, who had been so involved in her convincing arguments that she was sure she was gaining his agreement, gave him a confused frown. "Why not?''

"Because my great-uncle never gave or threw anything away except maybe the weekly kitchen trash. His house is a three-story nightmare of boxes, barrels, and bags of papers, books, broken furniture, you name it, and it's been sitting gathering dust since his death two years ago.''

Brittnie gulped. "It sounds bad.''

"It *is* bad."

"I have the feeling you're leaving something out."

"The truth is that no one knows exactly where the journals are. My grandfather himself says he hasn't seen them since sometime in the late sixties."

Brittnie felt the keen prick of disappointment, then accepted it. She was young enough to be dismayed at this glitch in her plans, but mature enough to know she could work around it. Her active mind began clicking over possible solutions to the problem. Hearing a faint sound, she turned a distracted glance toward the washroom. She saw nothing, so she returned her attention to Jared who was watching her reaction and waiting for her reply.

"So this could take weeks, or months," she said.

"Think in terms of years, Miss Kelleher. That's why I'm not sure you're the right person for the job."

"Why ever not?"

"Because you're young."

"And inexperienced," Brittnie said smartly. "Yes, we've established that. But just think, by the time I'm finished, I may be quite elderly and very experienced!"

Jared lifted a brow at her response and she bit her tongue, belatedly, as usual. She looked at him in distress. She didn't know what else to say to convince him except to add, "I can do the job. I'll work as efficiently as possible so you won't be paying me for taking coffee breaks. I promise that you can look in anytime and see how I'm doing."

"That won't be necessary," he responded in a dry tone. "My grandfather will be involved in the project and will oversee your work."

"Your grandfather wants to be involved in this?"

"Yes. He's very set on it." Jared didn't look any too happy about the idea. "Since his retirement, he's been restless and bored. Going through his older brother's papers will keep him occupied."

"I...see," Brittnie said cautiously. She wondered if Mr. Cruz had been trying to unretire himself by getting back into the family business. Jared didn't seem like the type to welcome that kind of interference.

"There is a catch, though."

"And that is...?"

"He's got a bad heart and has been warned against overwork."

Brittnie blinked at him. "So along with sorting and cataloging all the papers and searching for your great-grandmother's journals, I'm to be a nursemaid, too?"

Jared nodded. "That about covers it."

"Like hell," a gruff voice rumbled from the doorway of the washroom.

CHAPTER TWO

BRITTNIE and Jared spun toward the voice. A tall, thin man stood glaring at them. He had a shock of white hair and an indignant expression in his dark brown eyes.

"The last thing I need is a nursemaid," he said in a huffy tone as he stalked into the room. He waved a long, bony finger at Jared. "Send this girl packing, boy. I'll do the work myself."

Brittnie gasped in dismay, but Jared didn't seem perturbed by the man's outburst. Calmly, he said, "Hello, Granddad. Miss Kelleher, I'd like you to meet Roberto Cruz. Granddad, this is Brittnie Kelleher."

"I know who she is," Robert answered crossly. "Saw her name in that fancy notebook of yours."

"While you were sitting at my desk going through my accounts receivable, no doubt," Jared responded dryly, nodding toward the file drawer that had been left open.

Roberto didn't look at all guilty. Instead, he lifted his chin. "Just keeping my hand in, son. My name's on the door, you know."

"So is mine," Jared said. "Which is why I'm careful with the accounts."

Fascinated by this power struggle between the two men, Brittnie's head swung back and forth between them like a spectator at a tennis match. When Roberto didn't answer, she almost prompted him by saying, "Your shot." Instead, she bit the inside of her cheek to remind herself to keep her mouth shut.

The men stared at each other—Roberto red-faced and irritated, Jared calm and businesslike. Though his face didn't show it, Brittnie detected amusement and deep affection toward his grandfather.

"Miss Kelleher," Roberto said, turning to her and giving her a courtly, though stiff, bow. He fixed her with a gaze that was as direct as Jared's was. "No offense, but I have to agree with my grandson on this—you look too young for the job of sorting and classifying all the papers and other junk that David left behind."

Brittnie shot a quick glance at Jared. He lifted an eyebrow at her as if to confirm his agreement with Roberto. She shook her head and answered with an attempt at humor. "Will it help if I say I'll try to age very quickly?"

Jared frowned at her flip answer, but by now, she didn't care. She now seemed to be battling on two fronts and her first attempts at being diplomatic and businesslike hadn't worked.

Roberto surprised her by chuckling at her remark. "After you've seen the place, you'll know how true that may be."

She looked up to see that the older man was regarding her with a hint of respect in his eyes. He smiled and a moment of warm understanding flowed between them.

Roberto seemed to recall what he'd been saying and he frowned suddenly. "As for the other part of it—well, I damned well don't need a nursemaid." He bowed again, very slightly, from the waist. "Excuse my language."

In spite of his words, Brittnie found herself charmed by him. "Well, that's fortunate," she answered. "Because I'm not one."

Her gaze flew between the two men as she wondered

what would happen next. She hadn't bargained for this. Since the moment she'd heard about the job, she'd been obsessed with it. The idea of getting her hands on original material like the journals of Magdalena Cruz was a fond dream of hers. It had taken her a week to convince Jared's executive assistant, Sandra Bragg, to even consider her for the position, but she was nothing if not persistent and she'd worn the poor woman down. Her self-confidence had helped her breeze through the preliminary interview, which was how she'd landed this one with Jared. She had thought she would be willing to do almost anything to get this job, but—be a nursemaid? No, she hadn't bargained for that. And she certainly hadn't expected to meet opposition from yet another quarter.

She took a deep breath and looked at the man across the desk, then at his grandfather. Jared's dark eyes regarded her with interest, as if her answer to the two of them might affect her chances for the job.

"Don't you think it would be a good idea to hire a real nurse for him?" she asked hesitantly, giving the older man an apologetic look.

"You think I haven't tried?"

Roberto broke in. "I won't hear of it."

"Oh, you two have discussed it, then?"

"I've discussed many things with him lately." Jared's voice told her the discussions hadn't necessarily been pleasant ones.

Brittnie gave him a sharp glance as she recalled what he'd said a few moments before. His grandfather had grown restless and bored since his retirement. Did that mean he was trying to get back into the family business and Jared didn't want him? The older man's inspection of the accounts receivable file seemed to indicate as much. Brittnie thought it seemed cruel to exclude him from a business he'd built himself.

In the research she had done on Jared Cruz she had discovered that his reputation was that of being tough and direct—as he had been with Steve in the elevator—but not ruthless. Surely, he wouldn't be deliberately cruel to his own grandfather.

She glanced at the older man, who had taken the chair next to her and was watching her and Jared with sharp eyes.

There was an undercurrent of tension between the two men, as well as genuine affection, but in it, she sensed competition. She wondered if their problems stemmed from being too much alike and perhaps that was why Jared wanted Roberto occupied with his late brother's things and away from the office.

Brittnie gave herself a mental shake for the wild leaps her imagination was taking. She had no real basis to think of this man she'd just met. She was usually pretty good at reading people, but she couldn't quite put her finger on what motivated Jared Cruz.

She looked from Roberto to Jared and said, "Mr. Cruz, did you grant me this interview because you thought it would be easy to get me to act as nursemaid to your grandfather?"

Again, he lifted a brow slightly. "No. I granted the interview because you're highly recommended and since you grew up on a ranch, you must know something about hard work."

Brittnie shifted in her chair. He really *had* done his research if he knew that much about her. "Hard work, I know. Nursing, I don't know."

"There's no real nursing involved. You'll only have

to make sure my grandfather doesn't work too hard on this project."

"I know my own limitations, Jared, and I'll thank you to stop talking about me as if I wasn't sitting right here," the older man said, slapping his open palm on the arm of the chair.

Although she was having a hard time reading the situation between the two men, and how she fit into it, Brittnie had to admire Roberto's spirit.

Brittnie pictured her great-uncle Nate who, since he had turned eighty-five, seemed to spend most of his time napping in his chair. She couldn't imagine this man doing that, bad heart or no. In spite of the misgivings they both had about her role as nursemaid to him, she still wanted this job.

Growing up on a ranch had given her more than a healthy regard for hard work. She also knew a great deal about men—how to talk to them. She cast a glance at Jared. Well, some men, at least.

She turned to Roberto with a smile. "Mr. Cruz, I'm qualified to sort and classify your brother's letters and papers, but I'm not qualified to do more than that, so I can hardly be a nursemaid to you."

Some of the older man's prickly defensiveness seemed to abate. "Go on," he invited.

"I can look out for you, though, and we can work together on this." Her smile widened and her eyes twinkled with silvery lights. "You have to admit that the job will go better and more smoothly if you're there to tell me exactly what needs to be done."

This time Roberto responded with a smile of his own. "And that'll keep me out of my grandson's hair."

Brittnie nodded. "And out of his desk."

Roberto chuckled and reached over to pat her hand

lightly. "Jared, my boy, you've picked a sharp one here. She's willing to do what will please both of us." He sat back again and gave her a considering look. "In fact, you may have outsmarted yourself this time." He stood up and reached to shake her hand. He gave her a long, considering look. "You'll do, Brittnie. You'll do just fine. As far as I'm concerned, you've got the job as long as you don't try to take my pulse or my blood pressure."

"It's a deal, sir," she answered warmly, responding with a firm grip of her own.

Roberto turned to Jared. "It's settled, then. This is the girl you need, Jared. Work out the details. I've got a golf date." With that, he strolled from the room and shut the door.

Expectantly, Brittnie turned to Jared, but was stopped from speaking by the look on his face.

"Is...something wrong?" she asked cautiously.

"I'm trying to figure out this charm of yours."

She blinked at him. "What do you mean?"

"I'm wondering if you try to charm every man you meet, or if you have a special routine for the old ones." He rubbed his chin thoughtfully and his brows were drawn together in a straight line.

Brittnie pressed her lips together. No doubt, charm wouldn't work on this man, so she might as well be blunt. "Isn't it better to be charming to someone I'll be working with than to antagonize them from the outset?" When she realized it probably sounded as though she thought he was showing antagonism toward her, Brittnie shut her mouth.

He lifted an eyebrow at her. "I didn't necessarily mean that your charm is a bad thing."

Heat flushed her face. "Oh."

"In fact, it might be an asset. It will probably help

you out with my grandfather. He tends to be old-fashioned when it comes to women.''

Brittnie pressed her damp palms together. This didn't sound good at all. ''In what way?''

''You just played right into his hands with that talk of letting him be the boss. He thinks women need to be told what to do.''

Brittnie had the thought that it didn't take a genius to figure out it was a trait that seemed to run in the family. She eased the death grip her hands had on each other, took a breath, and tried to answer in a demure tone, which she knew was a stretch for her. ''Then I guess I'll have to be very diplomatic when he and I are working together.''

One corner of Jared's mouth edged upward. He leaned back in his chair and gave her another long look as if he was trying to decide if her statement had a double meaning. The expression on his face made him seem a little softer somehow, as if he was, for a moment at least, thinking of her as a person rather than a new employee— or as a potential pain in his side.

For a moment, Brittnie struggled to see him as her boss. She saw only a very attractive man who was looking at her as if he was trying to figure her out.

An odd tingling moved up Brittnie's arms. Had she been gripping the armrests so hard she had cut off the circulation?

''All right, Miss Kelleher,'' he finally said. ''You've talked your way into this job. You're certainly qualified. If my grandfather likes you and thinks you can do what's required, you're in. You have to expect him to be there to, well, *help* you.'' Jared emphasized the word as if wasn't sure how much help his grandfather would be.

Brittnie nodded. ''I understand.''

"Probably not, but you will soon. Remember, no matter what he thinks, part of your job is to keep an eye on him and make sure he doesn't work too hard."

In spite of her misgivings, Brittnie felt a swift surge of elation. She'd done it. She would be the first person in years, and the only professional archivist ever, to see the journals of Magdalena Cruz.

With a confident tilt to her chin, she held out her hand. "You can count on me, Mr. Cruz."

The look he gave her was as uncompromising as his handshake. "I'd better be able to, or you won't be long in this job."

Brittnie was about to say again that she understood, but when she looked into his eyes, all she could do was nod. She suddenly realized that he had no illusions about her. He wasn't sure she could do it, in spite of her high recommendations and obvious eagerness for the job. He hadn't seen her at her most professional that day, what with Steve's unwelcome pursuit of her, and Phil's comment about her suit. It was true that she could charm most people. Her mother swore she had started out practicing on her father and had him wrapped around her little finger by the time she was two days old.

Brittnie's glib tongue and ready laugh wouldn't work on this man, though. The firm grip of his fingers and the steadiness in his eyes told her as much.

He was wrong about her, though. There was far more to her than charm and she would prove it to him. She gave his hand an extra hard grip as she looked into his deep, dark, very skeptical eyes. "As I said, you can count on me."

"You need to celebrate." Brittnie's sister Shannon said in a decisive tone. She had stopped by the tiny apartment

Brittnie rented on the top floor of an old building to ask how the interview had gone. "After all, you're the last of the Kelleher women to become gainfully employed." She looked around disdainfully. "Now maybe you can move out of this place."

Brittnie grinned at her practical, down-to-earth older sister. "If a person isn't too fussy about heating, air-conditioning, and plumbing, this is a great place." Shaking out the jacket of Becca's blue suit, Brittnie placed it over the skirt, then hooked the hanger over the top of the bedroom door. "But don't worry, this is my last week here. The best part of this job is that I'll be able to live right in the house. Mr. Cruz's assistant has arranged the whole thing. See, I've already started packing."

Brittnie dragged a box of books from the bedroom into the tiny living room where Shannon sat on the one chair. She was still dressed for work in the jeans and long-sleeved denim shirt she wore for her job with the state. She was two years older than Brittnie, had black hair that reached nearly to her waist, and eyes that were the darkest shade of midnight blue. She was also extremely beautiful and she had to work hard to be taken seriously as a scientist in the office of soil conservation.

Brittnie grabbed a roll of packing tape and sealed the flaps of the box shut. Then she turned and sat on it. She pulled her T-shirt away from her throat and fanned herself as she stretched her long legs out before her. With one hand, she massaged the tired muscles of her thighs and calves through the denim of her jeans. She'd lost count of the number of times she'd made the trip up and down the endless flights of stairs to her car.

"And why is living in that house a good thing?" Shannon asked. "Didn't you just say the place has been closed up for two years? It's probably musty, dusty, and dreadful.''

"And rent free."

"Yeah, only a slumlord would charge you for the privilege of living with mice and roaches."

"I'll get a cat."

"You'll need one."

Brittnie laughed and glanced around the tiny studio apartment where she'd lived for several months while she had been working for the county library system. The place was stifling on this Indian summer day. "It can't be any worse than this. And besides, I don't mind camping out for a while. The money I save will go to pay off my college loans."

Shannon sighed. "I told you I've got some money saved now. I could pay those off for you."

"And then I'd owe the money to you instead. No thanks, I want to do this my own way."

"Just as you have since the moment of your birth," her sister responded in a resigned tone. "I can see why you would want to be on-site to work, but I'm still not crazy about the idea."

"You're sounding like a big sister," Brittnie responded. "This will work out fine. You know how involved I get when I'm researching. This way if I have one of my bouts of insomnia, I can get up and go to work until I'm sleepy. I'll be on my own schedule, work my own hours." She didn't know quite what kind of working relationship she was going to have with Roberto Cruz, but once she'd maneuvered her way past his crusty defensiveness, she'd thought he was a nice man which might translate into being a nice boss. She wished she could say the same thing for Jared Cruz. Nice was not a word she would ever apply to him. Disturbing would fit.

"It sounds good, I guess," Shannon answered slowly. "But I know you. You don't understand when to let something go. You'll probably stay up all night going through box after box of papers because you think there might be some little treasure of historical significance in one of them, then look around at six in the morning and wonder where the night went."

Brittnie laughed. "I'll try to control my obsessive habit."

"That'll be the day," Shannon sighed. She stood suddenly. "As I said, you need to celebrate, and I know just the way to do it. Ben and Timmy are in town. Let's go out."

Brittnie looked up in delight. Ben and Timmy Sills were their cousins who had spent the summer working in Denver for the Colorado Rockies baseball team. With the season ended, they were jobless, though they probably wouldn't stay that way for long. The two of them could turn their hand to anything from gourmet cooking to punching cattle.

"When did they get home?"

"Yesterday. How about it?"

Brittnie thought about all she needed to do in her hot apartment to get ready to move out within the next few days, then compared it to an evening of fun with her favorite cousins. No contest. Besides, Shannon had a tough job with an even tougher boss and she deserved some fun. "What time?"

Shannon headed for the door. "I'll go change and be back at seven. They'll pick us up here."

"You were pretty sure I'd go."

Shannon rolled her eyes. "I'm your big sister, remember? Besides," she said, taking on a sly, but excited look. "We've got something else to celebrate."

Brittnie caught the simmering excitement in Shannon's voice. "Oh, what's that?"

"I talked to Becca this morning. She and Clay had just come from the doctor's office. She's going to have another baby."

Brittnie jumped to her feet and crowed with delight. "That's wonderful. I've got to call her." She spun toward the phone, anxious to congratulate her oldest sister. Becca and Clay had been through some rough times, including a divorce and remarriage, but things seemed to be working out for them. No doubt her six-year-old nephew Jimmy was thrilled at the news, too. He'd said he either wanted a new baby or a new puppy.

"You'll have to call her later," Shannon said. "Clay was taking her and Jimmy out to celebrate. Now, head for the shower. It'll take half an hour to dry that hair of yours."

Brittnie gave her sister a sassy look as she strolled out, but did as she was told. Muttering about know-it-all big sisters, Brittnie hurried into the bathroom.

As it turned out, she didn't have time to dry her hair. The water pressure in the shower was more pitiful than usual so it took longer to wash it. By the time she was finished, she barely had time to put on her makeup, dress in a loose silver satin top and short black skirt, and fluff her hair out, leaving it to dry naturally. She knew it would be wild, but there was nothing to be done about it. She hurried downstairs to meet Shannon.

Ben and Timmy had friends who owned one of the finest restaurants in Durango, so the foursome managed to get in without reservations.

Talking excitedly about their summer with the baseball team, the boys led the way as they maneuvered
through the crowded dining room. At one point in their
journey across the room, Ben clasped Brittnie around the
waist and pulled her close as he finished the punchline
to a funny story.

Laughing, she half turned, and threw her head back.
Her gaze swept the room and met Jared Cruz's eyes.
Startled, she stopped suddenly and Ben barreled into her.
His arms shot out and wrapped around her to steady
them both.

Brittnie didn't even notice. Her attention was focused
on Jared, who was looking at her with interest and an
odd sort of challenge in his eyes. It was as if he was
asking what she was doing there. He placed his hands
on the table and half rose to his feet. Instantly, goose-
flesh popped out on her skin and heat washed through
her.

"Hey, Brittnie, what's the matter? You're holding up
traffic," Ben complained mildly.

"Oh, sorry," she gasped, glancing over her shoulder,
though she was barely able to focus on him. Responding
to the interest she'd seen in Jared's eyes, she said,
"Come over here for a minute. There's someone I'd like
you to meet."

She headed straight for Jared who stood and automatically straightened his suit jacket and the French
cuffs of his shirt. Brittnie noticed that he had changed
from the suit he'd worn earlier that day. This one was
black. It matched his hair, deepened the hue of his eyes,
and somehow made him appear cultured and yet dangerous.

His gaze ran over her, taking in the curls that cascaded
around her shoulders, her shimmering top and the skirt

that showed so much of her long legs. She curled her fingers into her palms to keep herself from bending her knees and tugging the hem of her skirt down.

"Good evening, Miss Kelleher," he said. "Celebrating your new job?"

Something in the expression in his eyes and the sound of his voice sent a flush of heat stirring through her. Her eyes widened in surprise at this unexpected reaction. Jared must have seen it because he focused on her, his own eyes narrowing with intensity. It was a full twenty seconds before Brittnie recalled the ring of people behind her. She managed to break her gaze away from Jared's and recall that he'd asked her a question. "Yes, I am." She turned blindly, wondering what on earth was coming over her, and introduced Shannon, Ben, and Tim.

"And this is Linda Pomfort," Jared said.

Startled because she hadn't noticed he was with someone, Brittnie blinked and glanced at the woman who was still seated at the table. She was petite, with rich auburn hair, eyes as green as emeralds, and a beautiful, creamy complexion. Stunning, Brittnie thought. The fixed expressions in her cousins' eyes told her they thought the same thing.

Jared gave the brothers a long, steady look, then focused on Ben, and the arm he had looped around Brittnie's waist, though Ben didn't appear to notice Jared's scrutiny. Brittnie saw it, though, and sent him a questioning look. He seemed to have taken an instant dislike to Ben. Defensively, she moved closer to her cousin and took his arm. He dragged his eyes from Linda long enough to give Brittnie a quick grin.

"How do you do?" Linda said. Her smile was cool

and reserved. "Jared says you're the one he's hired to sort his great-uncle's things."

"Yes," Brittnie answered, feeling her heart flutter at the idea that he'd been talking about her. "It should be…quite a challenge."

Standing before such compact beauty, Brittnie felt big and awkward. She glanced at Shannon who didn't seem at all affected by being faced with such perfection. Of course not, she thought sourly. Jared wasn't her boss. Shannon didn't care about impressing him the way…. Brittnie put the brakes on that thought. That was a path she was *not* going to let her thoughts take.

"Our table's ready," Ben said, gesturing to where the hostess hovered impatiently, though he gave Linda a reluctant look as he said it. She smiled back at him and he blushed.

"Oh, of course," Brittnie said, studying her cousin in surprise. She had never seen him blush before. "It was nice meeting you, Miss Pomfort," she said, her gaze skimming the other woman, then darting up to meet Jared's eyes. She was avidly curious to know the nature of their relationship, but fully realized it was none of her business.

She would also like to know the reason behind the severe looks he had been giving Ben. Surely he wasn't jealous of Ben's attraction to Linda. The two of them had barely met.

As if he could read what she was thinking, Jared's lips spread in a slow smile. "Good evening, then. It was nice seeing you."

Murmuring something equally innocuous, Brittnie turned with the others and moved away. So. Jared Cruz had a girlfriend, she thought as she sat down and accepted a menu from the hostess. She had known he wasn't married, but she hadn't given his status with the opposite sex any thought. Not that she should, she reminded herself. Studiously, she kept her eyes on the menu, reading the description of the prime rib dinner over and over.

Shannon leaned close, shielded her face behind her own menu, and whispered fiercely. "What on earth was *that* all about?"

Brittnie jerked and met her sister's eyes. "What?"

"The minute you saw him, you got the same look on your face you had the time Dad caught you smoking behind the barn. Guilty."

"Don't be ridiculous. I did nothing of the kind."

Shannon snorted inelegantly. "Maybe it wasn't guilt, but it was something. There were so many undercurrents flowing around there, if we'd been in a river we would have been sucked under."

Brittnie studied the menu and didn't meet Shannon's gaze. "I don't know what you're talking about. I didn't notice any undercurrents."

"Then you're not as smart as I always thought you were." Shannon turned to talk to Timmy. Brittnie concluded that her sister had been out in the sun too long that day. She ignored her. The next few minutes were occupied with ordering their meals.

When that was done, Brittnie excused herself and went into the ladies' room, hoping that she could use a comb and some hairspray to bring her hair under control. Barring that, she might take a cue from a lion tamer, and try a whip and chair. The image made her smile to herself.

When she swept in the door, her smile faded. Linda Pomfort was seated before a mirror, brushing her smooth, glistening hair. Brittnie automatically glanced at her own, which bounced merrily about her shoulders as if it was laughing at her attempts to tame it.

Linda looked up. "Oh, hello. Brittnie, isn't it?" She dropped her comb into her small evening bag and stood up.

"Yes." Brittnie paused awkwardly. The comparison between them was even worse than she thought. In her three-inch heels, Brittnie topped six feet and towered over the other woman.

"I don't envy you, working for Jared," Linda said suddenly.

What was this? Startled, Brittnie looked down to survey Linda carefully. "Oh? Why is that? Do you work for him?"

"Oh, no." Linda's beautiful green eyes gave Brittnie a look that asked if she was joking, then she glanced in the mirror and ran a hand over her perfectly smooth hair. "I don't work. I mean, I've heard he's a tough boss."

Brittnie stared at her as she fumbled around for an answer. She *really* didn't want to discuss Jared with his girlfriend. "I'm sure he's fair," she answered.

Linda greeted that with a tinkling laugh. "Oh, yes, he's fair, to a fault, I think. Sometimes he even hires people who aren't the least bit qualified just to give them a chance."

Brittnie could barely keep herself from laughing out loud. She didn't know Jared very well, but she doubted he could stay in business if he did very much of that. "Oh, really?" she said in a breathless tone.

"He's a true humanitarian." She gave Brittnie a quick, once-over look. "As long as his employees don't try and, well, overstep their bounds, and remember that they're just employees, after all. You'll remember that, won't you?"

Brittnie's jaw sagged. "Remember not to overstep my bounds?" she asked incredulously. Politeness be hanged. She couldn't let this one pass. "Miss Pomfort, an employee is exactly what I am. Not a servant—or a slave."

Linda's eyes widened for an instant and Brittnie thought she saw a flash of uncertainty, chased by fear, but it was gone in an instant. "Then you know your place," she said, recovering herself. "Good." She turned toward the door. "I'll be going. It was nice chatting with you."

She strolled out the door. As it swung silently shut, Brittnie continued to stare. She couldn't imagine what that had been about. Along with her surprise and irritation, Brittnie felt a pang of pity for the girl. She wondered why Linda felt she needed to put Brittnie in her place. Surely, she didn't think Brittnie was a threat to her? That Jared might develop a romantic interest in her? Brittnie could have reassured her on that point, but if that hadn't been what Linda had in mind, they both would have been embarrassed.

Dismissing the odd encounter, Brittnie moved to the mirror to work at controlling her hair. When she emerged from the ladies' room, she saw that Jared and his date had left.

Brittnie didn't even attempt to analyze the reason her gaze had swept the room looking for him or the disappointment that filled her when she didn't see him.

CHAPTER THREE

Two days later, Brittnie had the last of her things packed and ready to load into the pickup truck she had borrowed from her mother's ranch. Mary Jane Kelleher had said Brittnie could store her things in one of the outbuildings for the time being. For now, she would only take her clothes, toiletries, and the books and materials she knew she would need for the job.

It didn't take long for her to finish packing and to get the apartment cleaned up. After driving her things to the ranch and storing them in a shed, she indulged herself by going for a fast ride on her mare, Misty, because she knew it would be her last opportunity for a while, then she traded the pickup truck for her own car and returned to Durango.

Eagerly, Brittnie hurried to the offices of Cruz and Company to get the house key from Jared's assistant, Sandra Bragg. As she rode up in the elevator, she remembered the ride with Steve and Jared. Thankfully, Steve hadn't called or bothered her again. While she was grateful for that, she still wished the whole thing had never happened. It had colored Jared's opinion of her and she would have to work hard to change it. She rested against the side of the elevator and thought about the way his eyes changed from cool humor to hot irritation in a flash. She didn't particularly relish having either of those expressions turned in her direction and wondered what it would be like to have him look at her with admiration, affection, or even desire in his eyes.

When she realized the direction her thoughts were taking, Brittnie straightened suddenly. She must be truly tired if she was beginning to think of Jared Cruz in any romantic terms at all. The man was all-business, no-nonsense and he was her employer now. Besides, it appeared that he had a woman in his life. She'd do well to keep that in mind.

The elevator stopped at the fourth floor and she bustled into Sandra's office. Brittnie collected the key, and to her surprise, a laptop computer which Sandra said Jared insisted she would need. Brittnie was taken aback, touched by his thoughtfulness, though she knew better than to take it personally. From what she could see, all of his employees had the best available equipment to work with. Still, she was smiling when she left the office.

As she drove into the historic section of town, her excitement grew. She loved this area with its tall trees and stately homes. David Cruz's home, a few blocks from downtown was one of these Victorian treasures.

As she pulled up in front of the tall, red brick structure with white trim, Brittnie wondered why he had ever wanted such a huge home. In her research about the Cruz family, she had learned that he was a lifelong bachelor. He surely hadn't expected to fill the place up with a family because he'd bought it when he was in his fifties.

Brittnie turned off the motor, then leaned over the steering wheel of her car and stared up through the windshield. Although the place wasn't in the best of shape, it didn't look seriously neglected. And yet, there was an air about it of abandonment as if no one had really cared about it in a long, long time.

With a shrug, Brittnie stepped out. Looking up again, she concluded that David Cruz must have bought the place because he liked big, creepy-looking houses. Overgrown vines rattled their branches against the walls and scratched at the windows which stared out onto the surrounding mountains with big, vacant eyes.

Brittnie gave herself a shake. She was being ridiculous. It was true that she had an overactive imagination, but there was no point in scaring herself to death before she got inside. Sure, the house looked deserted, but that didn't mean there was anything frightening inside, she told herself heartily. Besides, *she* was the one who had suggested she live on-site. Jared had been reluctant to let her do it, but she had finally convinced him by saying that the property would be better off with a caretaker.

She straightened her shoulders and reached for the door. She had asked for it, and now she had it.

Creaking and groaning sounds in the old house brought Brittnie awake with a start. Her heart jumped into her throat and lodged there as she sat bolt upright on the bed. She heard a faint popping sound as if the wooden floorboards were easing their joints and settling in for the night. Relieved to realize they were the normal sounds that the old place probably made every night, Brittnie placed her hand to her throat to calm her heartbeat, then scooted to the edge of the bed and dangled her feet over. She brushed her tangle of hair back from her face, then rubbed her eyes as she squinted at the clock she had placed on the bedside table.

Ten o'clock. Midnight might be a more appropriate hour to be awakened by creepy sounds, but ten was bad enough. Exhausted from the move, she had collapsed across the bed at eight o'clock, intending to rest for a few minutes, but she had fallen asleep.

Brittnie pushed herself to her feet, knowing she had

to shower and prepare for bed, though her ridiculously late nap would probably make sleep impossible. She did some groaning of her own when her leg muscles cramped in protest to the hard workout she'd been giving them the past few days.

With a hobbling stagger, she made her way into the bathroom which was attached to the room she had chosen for herself. She thought it must have been David Cruz's bedroom. She had chosen it because it was relatively free of the boxes, cartons, barrels, and crates of items that crowded the house. She'd thought Jared had been joking about the collections of things that crowded the place, but as soon as she'd walked in, she'd learned that he had been all too serious. It would take years to go through it all.

Telling herself that she would at least have job security, she stepped into the shower. She washed her hair, then let the hot water wash over her until her muscles loosened up a bit. By the time she had dried off and pulled on underwear and the outsize man's T-shirt she wore for a nightgown, she felt almost normal except for the raging hunger that was giving her a headache and making her stomach growl.

Thinking of the groceries she had stored in the kitchen, Brittnie headed from the room. She was halfway down the hall before she realized there was light coming from downstairs. She frowned, sure that she'd turned all the lights off before going up to find a bedroom.

She moved to the top of the staircase and placed her hand on the newel post. A faint sound reached her. It wasn't the creaking and groaning of the old house that she'd already heard. This was a scraping noise as if someone was moving something. Goose bumps ran up her arms and tingled across her shoulders.

She was no longer alone in the house.

Frantically, Brittnie tried to recall exactly where the telephone was located. She knew it was still connected, but in this house, it was probably buried under piles of junk. Unless...

She paused, her heart pounding in her throat. Most people had a phone in the kitchen. Had David Cruz had one there? Why not? she thought hysterically, he had everything else in there. She would look in the kitchen even though it meant trying to creep past the living room where she thought the burglar probably was.

As she edged silently toward the staircase, she kept her breathing shallow and even. It wouldn't do for her to hyperventilate, faint, and fall down the stairs. She could handle this if she stayed calm.

The house had been sitting empty for two years. Why did a burglar pick tonight to break in? she wondered as she made her cautious way to the staircase. And what was he trying to steal, anyway? Boxes of papers? A broken bicycle wheel? The empty mayonnaise jars that lined the living room window?

Brittnie stood on the top step, curling her bare toes over the edge as she tried to remember what she'd learned in the self-defense class she had taken a few years ago in college. It had been a requirement for all freshman girls and she thought she probably remembered enough, but still, she wished she had a weapon— or even a rope. She'd grown up on a ranch. She knew how to rope—and how to tie a calf for branding.

She wasn't a violent woman, but she would be awfully glad of a baseball bat or a fireplace poker right now. Her advantage would be surprise if there was a confrontation, but with any luck, she could find the phone and call the police before the burglar even knew she was in the house.

On the other hand, she thought, there might not be any need for violence. Once the burglar caught sight of her, and the wild look in her eyes, he might decide he'd happened on a crazy woman and flee without a fight.

Treading lightly to minimize the squeaking of the stairs, Brittnie stole down to the landing. All the lights were blazing in the front hall and in the living room. Before she turned toward the kitchen, she stopped, blinking in the brightness.

What kind of burglar turned on all the lights?

On tiptoe, she moved to the archway that led to the living room and flattened herself, face-first, against the wall as she'd seen detectives do in numerous action movies. As she did so, she heard a faint grunt, as if someone had lifted something heavy. Curious, she moved her head sideways just enough for her left eye to get a view of the room, and came eyeball to eyeball with Jared Cruz who was walking toward the doorway.

With a shriek, she leaped back.

"Hey!" Jared shouted, dropping the box he'd been carrying. It landed on his foot. "Yeow!" he shouted again and did a one-legged hop around the room.

Brittnie shrieked again and clutched her hand to her throat. "What in the world are you doing here?" she gasped, her eyes huge and startled as she watched him come to rest against the back of a wing chair. "You scared me to death."

"Well, excuse me, but you're something of a surprise yourself," Jared shot back, breathing deeply and grimacing. With one hand he rubbed his foot, and with the other, he stabbed a finger toward her nose. He swallowed and then said, "What are you doing sneaking around here?"

"I'm not sneaking," she insisted. "I'm supposed to be able to live here while I do the job you hired me to do. Remember? You arranged it."

"You weren't supposed to move in here until later in the week."

"So...so I moved in early. Sandra knows I'm here." Brittnie clapped her hands onto her hips. "Being here early doesn't mean you can...terrorize me."

"I haven't talked to Sandra." He gave Brittnie a skeptical look. "Terrorize? I think you're being melodramatic."

She huffed indignantly. "All right then, you frightened me. I thought you were a burglar."

Jared glanced around with an astounded look. "What burglar in his right mind would *want* any of this stuff?" He put his foot down and took an experimental step as if to make sure it wasn't broken. He breathed a sigh of relief even as he gave her a harried look.

In spite of her lingering fright, Brittnie felt her lips twitch. "I wondered the same thing, but I thought I'd let the police ask that question." She lifted her hands. "But I guess there's no reason to call them now."

"I hope not," Jared said, then he paused. His gaze traveled over Brittnie's hair which hung around her face in ringlets and was dampening the shoulders of her T-shirt. His eyes met the startled brightness in hers and noted the color in her cheeks, then narrowed as he noticed the briefness of her T-shirt and her bare legs.

Suddenly remembering that the T-shirt hit her only at mid-thigh and that she had on very little under it, Brittnie crossed her arms over her chest and placed one foot on top of the other. Heat washed through her and she could feel a blush climbing her throat.

Some malevolent star in the heavens was shining down on her again. She could almost feel its beams hitting squarely on her head. Here she was nearly nude, and he was dressed in one of his usual corporate suits and ties, though this time, the tie was loosened and his top shirt button open. Brittnie caught herself noticing the bronze skin of his throat, the faint stubble of his beard, and the tiredness that rimmed his eyes. It all came together to make him seem incredibly sexy and heart-breakingly tired.

Jared's eyes came back up to meet hers. "Is the owner of that shirt waiting for you upstairs?"

"*What?*"

"I mean that cowboy you were with the other night."

Brittnie blinked, trying to think who he meant. "You mean Ben?"

Jared's dark eyes turned cool. "If that's his name. Your private life is your own business, but this house is still property owned by my family."

All kinds of possibilities darted through Brittnie's mind. Why would he be interested in her private life? In her "boyfriend"? "And you don't want me having any, um, overnight guests?" She knew she shouldn't bait him, but he was presenting a challenge she couldn't ignore.

"Not particularly." Jared crossed his arms over his chest. "Should I have made that part of my agreement when I said you could stay here?"

"No. I rarely have overnight guests, male or female. Besides, Ben says I snore, or at least that's what he told me about fifteen years ago."

"Fifteen…?"

"When I was ten and he was eight and our families went camping together. You see, Ben is my cousin. Even if he wasn't, he wouldn't be interested in being my boyfriend, because he says I'm too bossy."

Jared's lips twitched. "So can I assume you didn't get that T-shirt from an old boyfriend?"

"Humph, that's quite a leap of a conclusion," she said with an upward glance. "But you seem to be good at that." Too late, she bit her lip. It was a measure of how mentally stimulated she felt when around him that she even had the nerve to make such a statement.

"So I've been told."

"I buy them three in a package at the department store."

"Not that it's any of my business," he supplied.

"And…and I don't think that's any kind of a question for a boss to be asking an employee—even one who's living in his house, or a house owned by his family," she finished up with a firm nod.

Jared laughed, but there was no humor in it. "Brittnie, I think that whole boss/employee thing got blown out the window the first few minutes we were together in that elevator."

Brittnie glanced away, uncomfortably recalling the scene with Steve and the whopper she'd told about Jared being the man in her life. Of course, then she hadn't known about Jared and Linda Pomfort, who was obviously the true woman in his life.

"Brittnie, have you got a robe?"

"Yes, of course." Did he think she ran around like this all the time, enticing unsuspecting men to their doom? she wondered sourly.

"Why don't you go put it on? Then if you'll help me with these boxes, I'll get out of here." He turned and indicated several he had pulled out of the mess and stacked on the living room side of the archway.

"What exactly are you doing, anyway?" she asked, with a frown.

"Years ago, my uncle was the legal representative for Cruz and Company. I'm taking some of the old legal papers that have to do with my company. He stored them here, but they have nothing to do with his personal papers, so I'm going to take them to the office."

Brittnie's gray eyes grew skeptical. "And you had to come over at midnight to do this?"

"I just got back into town," he said. "I knew I wouldn't be able to sleep, so I decided to come take care of this now."

"I see." Brittnie said. "Well, then I'll go and...I'll be right back." Her hands fluttered when she realized she couldn't shield her front and her behind, too.

She backed toward the stairs and when he turned to the living room, she whirled around and hurried up to her room. No way was she returning downstairs in her robe, which didn't reach much further than the T-shirt. Besides, it had loose sleeves which were a hazard in the kitchen. After she helped Jared load his boxes and she got him on his way, she was going to fix herself something to eat and didn't want to wear the robe while using that old kitchen range.

Instead she dressed quickly in jeans, a long-sleeved flannel shirt, socks and loafers, reasoning that if she helped carry those boxes out to his car, she would need protection from the cold night air. So what if she looked like a lumberjack? In the bathroom, though, she considered her makeup kit, then grabbed her mascara and swiped some across her lashes, then highlighted her cheeks with dusky rose blush. Even lumberjacks had some pride of appearance, she thought, finishing up with a dab of lipstick. She considered perfume, but thought that would be carrying things too far.

She hurried back down to help and found that he had already begun loading the boxes in his car, a four-wheel-drive utility vehicle. She smiled when she saw it through the open door. Considering the way he dressed, and the kind of man he seemed to be, she would have expected him to drive a sports car. This was a pleasant surprise.

"Something's funny?" Jared asked, coming up behind her with yet another carton in his arms. He had removed his suit jacket and rolled up his shirt sleeves. The muscles in his forearms flexed as he hefted the box against his stomach, where there wasn't the slightest hint of a paunch.

Brittnie opened her mouth to answer, but she looked down and wondered suddenly if all men had such attractive arms or if she'd just never seen it before. She couldn't believe she hadn't noticed the way dark hair looked against smooth, coppery skin. She had been around men all her life; her father, cousins, ranch hands, the boys she grew up with, boyfriends over the years. She couldn't recall noticing such a detail as their forearms before, though.

Jared wasn't like the men she knew well. She doubted that he did much physical work, but in spite of that, he seemed so very masculine.

What would it feel like to touch his arms, to run her fingers over those tough muscles and sift them through the hair there. Would it be as soft as down, or maybe as soft as cat's...?

"Brittnie?" Jared's voice brought her slightly glazed eyes up to meet his. "Something's funny?"

"Furry," she said faintly.

"What?"

His astounded exclamation snapped her out of her daydream. "It's, uh, nothing," she sputtered. "I was only thinking that—" Her face flushed bright red. "Nothing," she finished lamely.

Just then, her stomach growled. Loudly. "I'm hungry," she said hastily. "Faint from hunger, in fact. I don't know what I'm saying." She winced when she realized what had just popped out of her mouth. No doubt, he would answer that it seemed to be a chronic condition with her. Her sister Becca said that Brittnie was the fast thinker in the family. That ability seemed to have deserted her. "I was going to fix myself a sandwich or something." Or several sandwiches, once he was gone.

His dark eyes lit up and he surprised her by grinning in such a teasing and boyish way that Brittnie slumped helplessly against the doorjamb while heat sifted down and pooled in her stomach. This was crazy and getting crazier by the minute. In fact, she was having strange reactions to him that were getting way out of hand.

"Then why don't I take you out and feed you?"

Spend even *more* time with him, thinking these dangerous thoughts? She shook her head and answered in a brisk tone. "That really isn't necessary, thank you."

"It's no trouble. I'm hungry, too."

"I'd prefer to eat here."

He put his hands on his hips and thrust his jaw forward. "Are you *always* this stubborn?"

"I'm not stubborn," she said haughtily. "Just determined."

"Look, I interrupted your dinner, so I feel responsible for feeding you."

She opened her mouth to say she couldn't imagine

why, but the determined expression on his face had her snapping it shut. He was right. She was being stubborn.

"There are a couple of restaurants around that are open twenty-four hours a day," he went on. "Of course, I'm not guaranteeing the quality."

Her stomach growled again and she clapped her hands over it. "At this point, I think quantity is more important," she admitted.

His grin grew into a chuckle. "Then let's go. We can finish loading these things when we get back."

He gently took her arm, but she held back.

"Uh, there's one other thing," she said, giving him an unhappy look. "I would really rather pay for my own meal."

"That's not necessary," he said briskly. "I was the one who invited you, remember?"

"Yes, but I may not be the kind of person you want to take to a public restaurant."

"Why? Do you eat soup with your hands?"

She rolled her eyes. Brittnie knew she was going to sound foolish when she said this, but the man deserved fair warning. "No, of course not, but I eat a lot."

His eyebrows rose. "Excuse me?"

She threw her hands in the air, dislodging his hold on her elbow. "Look at me, Mr. Cruz…Jared. I'm nearly six feet tall. I work hard. It takes a lot of food to fill me up and—" She shrugged. "I guess I have a very fast metabolism, because I get hungry often and I haven't eaten since this morning."

This time his grin grew to an outright laugh. "And I'll bet you've been teased about it your whole life."

Her smile quirked. "Yes, I have. I had one boyfriend who told me I'd missed my calling. I should have been a lumberjack."

Jared plucked at the sleeve of her flannel shirt. "Looks like you're dressed for the part." He took her arm. "Did it ever occur to you that maybe you're just picking the wrong boyfriends?"

Brittnie bit her tongue. Why hadn't she just said "someone" had made the lumberjack comment?

He must not have expected an answer to his question because he went on, "Don't worry about it, Brittnie. Maybe you haven't heard, but I'm a rich man. I can afford it. If it looks like my bank balance can't handle the strain, I've got friends I can hit up for a loan."

Brittnie laughed, surprised that he could joke about it. She hadn't expected that from him, but then, she didn't know him, although she suspected he didn't often go out to eat with women who devoured food the way she did. She already knew that women like Linda with reed-slim figures and—no doubt—tiny appetites were his usual dates. Not that this was a date, she reminded herself.

On the heels of that thought came the memory of her strange conversation with Linda Pomfort. For several days now, she had pondered Linda's oddly fearful possessiveness. In spite of her curiosity, though, she wouldn't tell him about her conversation with Linda, or ask about his relationship with her. That would be, as Linda would have said, far beyond Brittnie's "bounds."

Jared hustled her outside, closed and locked the door behind them and directed her toward his car. Brittnie followed along as he took charge, a rarity for her. She had been born a leader and had been busy polishing up that character trait ever since. If someone had asked why she was going along with Jared so meekly, she could only have said that he intrigued her. When he placed his hands at her waist to help her into the seat, her heart surprised her by doing a slow, soft roll in her chest. He also attracted her.

Who would have thought, that after their uncomfortable first meeting, he would turn out to be so considerate? Maybe it proved the truth of the old saying about the unreliability of first impressions. Brittnie gave him a quick, sideways look as he climbed into the car, fastened his seat belt, started the engine, and checked his rearview mirror.

She didn't have to guess what his first impression had been of her. The scene with Steve had led him to think she had any number of men—if she could judge by his question about her T-shirt and his remark that she picked the wrong boyfriends.

They had started out on the wrong foot and she wished there was some way to correct things. Maybe having a midnight meal together would help. Her stomach growled yet again. On second thought, maybe the only thing that would be helped would be her appetite.

Jared pulled into an all-night restaurant with a parking lot empty of cars. Inside, they were the only patrons and were shown to a booth by a waitress who didn't look overjoyed to have customers in her empty place. Moving at a snail's pace, she brought them glasses of water, then headed toward the kitchen.

Once she and Jared were seated on opposite sides of the table, Brittnie plucked the menu from its holder and looked it over. She was famished and everything looked wonderful, though she knew the photographs of the food on the menu probably wouldn't bear the slightest resemblance to the actual dish once it was prepared. She didn't care. If that waitress didn't hurry, Brittnie thought she might just eat the menu itself.

Anxiously, she looked in the direction of the kitchen

where, by now, the waitress had been for several minutes. Jared caught her glance. Immediately, he stood and called out, "Excuse me. Could we have some service over here?"

Responding to his commanding tone, the waitress hustled out, her pad and pen ready. "Yes, sir," she said breathlessly.

Jared ordered a sandwich and Brittnie, with a longing look at the menu, ordered one, also. He gave her a retiring look and said, "I thought you were hungry."

"Well, yes, but...."

"She'll have two of those, a double order of French fries, and a double of coleslaw." He took the menu from Brittnie, flipped it shut, and slipped it back into its holder. "We'll order dessert later," Jared finished.

"Yes, sir." The waitress hurried away.

Brittnie placed her hands on top of the table, laced her fingers together loosely, and gave him a grateful look. "You're a pal. Thanks for being so...."

"Pushy?"

"Understanding," she said, then added, "And pushy."

He tilted his head in one of those masculine gestures that Brittnie had so often seen her father do when he was satisfied with something. "My pleasure."

Her pleasure was looking at him. He really did have the most beautiful eyes; dark and full of life, interested in what was going on around him. Even now, they traversed the room, examining the unimaginative decor. She knew he must be exhausted, but he sat up straight, his back barely touching the vinyl booth. He seemed to be a man of character and stamina. She already knew he had integrity. Too bad he had a tendency to make snap judgments.

The waitress must have inspired the cook with some of Jared's urgency, because their meals arrived in record time. Brittnie couldn't even pretend to make polite conversation while she ate. She tucked into her meal and devoured everything in sight.

Jared finished long before she did and sat sipping his coffee and watching her.

When she finished, she sat back, pushed her plate away, and said, "Don't say I didn't warn you."

"I wouldn't dream of it."

She propped her elbow on the table, looked at her empty plate, and said, "You know, if my metabolism ever slows down, I'll be in serious trouble."

One corner of his mouth lifted and his gaze roamed over her. "You could stand a few more pounds."

Brittnie blinked and looked down at her hands, then up to meet his eyes.

"What's the matter?" he asked.

"I shouldn't say things that invite personal comments like that."

"Why not?"

"That's how I got into that...situation with Steve Wilberson." Her face flushed as she admitted it.

His laugh was derisive. "And you think *you* were wrong?"

Her hands flipped in a helpless gesture. "I must have said something that set him off."

"A guy like that doesn't need anything to set him off except maybe the approach of his fortieth birthday."

She sat back. "Oh. I hadn't thought of that. He could be having a midlife crisis. Or a case of the seven-year itch?"

"Yep."

"Poor Lauren," Brittnie murmured. "I wonder how long it will take him to get over it."

"He'll probably get over it at exactly the same second she finds out about it."

Brittnie smiled even though she felt sorry for her friend. After a moment, she said, "Jared, I told such an outrageous lie in the elevator...." Her smile faded as she thought about it. "Why did you back me up?"

"Because you looked mad enough to mop up the floor with him and it was pretty crowded in there. I didn't want to be on the receiving end of your fist if you swung at him and missed."

Her lips twitched. "Seriously. Tell me why."

He sobered, shrugged, and said, "You looked like you needed help."

She laughed. "I hardly look like a damsel in distress."

"Do you think that just because you're nearly six feet tall, and were raised on a ranch doing hard work, that you should be able to handle every situation?"

"I...I guess I never thought of it that way," she answered slowly.

"Everyone needs help sometimes."

She nodded in agreement but she wondered how often he received help he hadn't paid for, or if he was the one always giving the help. She didn't know him well enough to ask such a question so she searched around for a neutral subject, then noticing the coffee he was drinking, asked, "Won't that keep you awake?"

He shrugged. "Nah. When I'm tired enough I just crash, caffeine or no."

"You do that, too? I thought I was the only one. That's why I was anxious to actually live on site in your uncle's house. I can work when I'm having a bout of insomnia and get much more done."

"Doubtless you'll have many years' worth of insomnia in that place, and nightmares. Now that you've seen the house, do you understand what I was trying to tell you?"

Brittnie propped her elbow on the table and sighed. She ran both hands through her long hair, pushing it away from her face, but the curly tendrils sprang back as soon as she released them. "You were absolutely right. I've never seen anything like it in my life."

"I guess you haven't seen the garage yet, then, hmm?"

She groaned and covered her eyes. "There's more?"

"Well, if you think you can't handle it...." Jared said, letting his voice trail off.

Brittnie snapped to attention. "I can handle it," she answered indignantly before she saw that his eyes were smiling at her. She settled back. "Tell me about your great-uncle. Was he a collector?"

"No, he just couldn't seem to get rid of anything. I think he felt he had to keep everything people gave him." Jared went on to tell her about David's career in law and the people he had helped. During the Depression, he had been a young attorney with a struggling practice and a hunger for justice. Most of his clients had been poor farmers or farm laborers who had been unable to pay him in anything except goods. Many of these things were items he couldn't really use, but he'd saved them.

"You'll probably still find them somewhere in that mess," Jared said.

Brittnie's eyes lit up. "Social history," she said. "Mementos of the Depression era."

"Mess," he answered in a dry tone.

She wrinkled her nose at him. "I'll bet the historical society could use some of those things."

Jared shook his head. "Another collector. Sounds like you and my great-uncle would have been kindred spirits." He stood, counted several bills onto the table, and waited while she slipped from the booth and joined him. They walked slowly from the restaurant and into the cool night.

In spite of the cold, Brittnie was beginning to feel sleepy, but somehow satisfied. The two of them hadn't really talked about anything significant, but she felt she knew him a little better.

She wanted to know even more. Curiosity about him had teased her since the moment they had met. His origins were as rooted to the land as her own, and yet he had an air about him of cosmopolitan grace, the elegant style she had noticed right away. She didn't know any other men like him.

CHAPTER FOUR

THE ride back to David Cruz's overcrowded house was quiet. She certainly didn't know what Jared was thinking, but Brittnie found herself dwelling on the fact that her new employer was a very attractive man. This disturbed her because she didn't want to notice that and be distracted by it.

When they arrived home, Jared walked her to the front door. She had left the porch light on and in its harsh yellow glow, he looked tired.

"I won't keep you, Mr....uh, Jared. Thank you for dinner. You saved my life."

His lips twitched. "Well, we do seem to have tamed that tiger that was growling away inside you."

"For now," she sighed.

Jared nodded, then his face grew grave. "Brittnie, my grandfather will start coming over in a day or two."

"Oh?" She chewed her lip anxiously. She had hoped to have a little more time to work alone and get things organized before he joined her. From the looks of things, though, it would take her weeks to get organized.

"He lives out by the golf course and the drive will be hard on him, but he insists."

Brittnie frowned. "That's not a difficult drive."

"That's what he tells me." He glanced at her, then out into the darkness of the quiet street. "You're thinking that I'm taking overprotectiveness much too far."

Brittnie blinked because that was exactly what she had been thinking.

"He's...important to me," Jared said slowly. He didn't look at her again and Brittnie wondered if he was reluctant to show the depth of his emotions to a woman he barely knew, or if, like most men, he had been conditioned by circumstances and by society to keep his emotions under control.

"You don't want anything to happen to him," she offered.

"No, I don't and I'm going to do everything in my power to make sure it doesn't."

Even going so far as to enlist her aid in looking out for Roberto. Although she felt she should probably be getting extra pay for nurse duties, Brittnie said, "I'll watch him. Surely it won't be that difficult to get him to sit down with one of these boxes and sort the contents."

"You don't know my grandfather."

"I can handle it," Brittnie said with more confidence than she felt. "Don't worry. I can be tough."

"Well, if you do your job, I won't have to worry," he said in a cool tone.

Miffed because she had thought there was a measure of understanding between them, Brittnie answered. "I'll do the job for which I'm paid, no matter how long it takes and no matter how hard it is."

"Then things should work out fine."

Brittnie's warm feelings toward him evaporated. This man was too complicated for her to figure out tonight. She was tired. With a weary sigh, she turned to go into the house. "Why don't we load those boxes into your car and you can be on your way."

He nodded in agreement as he followed her inside. They quickly packed eight boxes in his Jeep and he said he would return for the others in a few days.

She stopped him before he got out the door. "Mr.—I mean, Jared. You hired me to organize your great-uncle's papers and letters. In other words, to be a librarian and an archivist."

"That's right."

"Thanks for the use of the laptop. It'll make the job easier."

"That was the intention."

"I appreciate that but...." She waved her hand at the messy house. "I'm not a cleaning lady."

He lifted an eyebrow at her. "Well, if you were, you'd be the highest paid one I've ever known."

Brittnie ignored that. "This job will go much faster if I don't have to cart away all this unnecessary stuff."

"You're saying you need help?"

"At least someone to haul off things like that," she said, pointing to the mayonnaise jars that lined the windowsill.

"Maybe Uncle David planned to sprout some sweet potatoes. And with him, if one jar was good, twenty were a whole lot better."

"Well, in this case, he had too much of a good thing."

Jared moved toward the front door as he said, "I'll see what I can do about getting you some help."

"Thank you," she said, ready to close the door. "Good night, Mr....I mean, Jared."

"Better work on calling me by my first name, Brittnie. We're going to know each other for a long time." He paused and look at her for a long moment.

Brittnie wondered what he was seeing; a woman who dressed, and ate, like a lumberjack, the professional archivist she was striving to be, or someone suffering the conflicts of having met an attractive man who was unavailable and who expected things from her she wasn't sure she could do.

She met his gaze hesitantly, then straightened in surprise at what she saw there. His eyes focused on her face for a moment, then swept down her body. She felt a rush of warmth pass through her as if he had touched her. She couldn't quite read what was in his eyes, but she thought it was interest which made her heart pound. His face grew shuttered then, as if his thoughts were folding in on themselves, keeping his secrets.

Brittnie lifted a hand to him, though she didn't know what she intended to say except, "Jared?"

"That's better." His approval came in a tone much smoother than she had managed. "We're going to know each other for a long time, and very well." Leaving her fumbling with her confusion of thoughts, he sketched a wave in the air and returned to his Jeep. Brittnie closed and locked the front door and then leaned against it.

She wasn't sure if that had sounded more like a statement or a promise.

In spite of her late-night supper with Jared, and her excitement over the job that had kept her awake, Brittnie was up and eager to work early the next morning. Her first priority was to clear a space in which to work. The most logical area was the downstairs dining room because of the mahogany table, spacious enough to seat twelve comfortably. She could spread out her work, set up the laptop, and have enough room for any reference materials she might need.

She stood in the doorway to the kitchen, gazing at the table as she sipped her morning coffee and wondered if David Cruz had ever entertained such a large number of people and what they had thought of his overstuffed house. She had been in the house for less than twenty-four hours, but she knew that the more she learned about David Cruz, the more he intrigued her. After what Jared had told her about him and his law practice, she knew he had been more than just a pack rat.

She imagined him with the courtly manners that Roberto Cruz displayed—or at least he had displayed them after she got past his prickly manner. Would Jared be like that when he was in his eighties, she wondered—decisive and full of self-assurance? Probably, she concluded. He was that way now.

Realizing her thoughts were starting down the same path that had occupied much of the night, Brittnie set her cup down in the kitchen sink, rubbed her hands together, and started to work. She had just hauled the first few boxes out of the dining room when a cleaning crew arrived. She was pleased that Jared had been true to his word, and in record time.

By the time the crew left three days later, the house was almost livable with mountains of old things hauled away for discard or recycling and all the containers of papers and books that had been located so far stacked in the dining room. She sighed when she looked at it. The room looked like a bunker expecting a direct hit from a weapon of mass destruction, but at least she had a place to work. There was a library on the far side of the entryway with floor-to-ceiling bookcases, a fireplace, desk, and comfortable wing chairs.

It was a librarian's paradise. She knew instinctively that this was where David Cruz had spent much of his time. She was anxious to explore it, but there was still a great deal to be done in the other rooms first.

Roberto Cruz arrived for work the next morning. He

was dressed in a natty blue blazer, tan slacks and a white golf shirt. He looked trim and healthy and Brittnie had a hard time believing there was anything wrong with him. She had been kneeling on the floor, going through a carton of file folders with dates from the nineteen fifties. Standing quickly, she dusted the knees of her jeans.

"Hello, Mr. Cruz."

"Brittnie." He nodded at her, then looked around. Though still cluttered, the place was clean and it was possible to get around without falling over things. "You must have some kind of magic touch."

"I wish I could take credit for it, but the credit goes to your grandson."

Roberto looked at her over the top of his sunglasses. "You can't convince me he's been over here with a mop and a broom."

She burst out laughing and told him about the crew Jared had hired.

"Good for him," the older man said. "It should have been done months ago, but Jared was busy and I didn't feel like tackling it alone." He took off his jacket, folded it over the back of one of the freshly dusted and polished chairs and said, "Looks like it's time for me to get to work, though."

"Oh, okay." Brittnie looked around vaguely. She'd been expecting this, but now she didn't know quite where to start.

"I know you said I could be the boss here while we're working together, but why don't we work out a compromise?"

"Compromise?" she asked uncertainly.

"Yeah. You be the boss today, and tomorrow we'll pretend that I'm the boss." He lifted his arm and flexed his muscles. "That way, I can maintain my macho image."

She laughed again, liking him more each time she met him. "We certainly want to keep your image intact, so let's get started." She pointed to the promising-looking cartons that she and the cleaning crew had collected from the rest of the house and moved into the room. "The first thing we need to do is organize these as closely as we can by year, then we'll go through each one and catalog the contents."

"All right, boss." Roberto pulled a chair beside a box, sat down and started working.

Before long, Brittnie discovered six volumes bound in green cloth. When she realized they were diaries that David had kept from his service in World War I, her heart nearly stopped. So, Magdalena Cruz hadn't been the only member of the family to record personal history. What a treasure.

Reverently, she opened the one dated early in 1915 and read a few lines. Her eyes blurred when she saw that the pages were cross-written; written across the page in the normal manner, then turned and written from the bottom to the top so that the writing intersected. She knew people had done this to save paper, but it made the writing as hard to read as a scribbled checkerboard. Standing, she carried the first diary over to Roberto.

"I wondered if David still had these," he said as he took it and opened the cover. "I guess I should have known better. I was aware that he had kept a diary during those years."

"Maybe it was a habit he learned from your mother."

"Maybe, but later he never talked about them, or about his war service, so I thought these were long gone. He was seventeen when he enlisted. Ran away from home and lied about his age. I was only three, but I remember that Mother was furious with him. She wore holes in the rug by her bed praying for him until he came home safely.'' Roberto touched the cover reverently. "I want to read these."

"Look at the writing," Brittnie suggested. "You might want to wait until I can transcribe them."

Roberto examined the first few pages, then shook his head and handed the diary back, disappointment and regret lining his face. "You're right. Even after cataract surgery, my old eyes can't read this. I'll wait." He gave her a quick grin. "But I might not have much time, so hurry."

Her answering smile had a sad little catch to it, but she promised that she would. Carefully, she put the diary back with its fellows, marked the carton appropriately, and went on to the next one.

Soon afterward, Roberto grew tired and began to sag in his chair. Alarmed, Brittnie suggested that he lie down in the living room, but he insisted that he could drive home. She watched with a worried expression as he drove away, but she could see that he was extremely careful. As she returned to the house, she wondered why Jared didn't hire a driver for his grandfather. Probably for the same reason he didn't hire a nurse. Roberto wouldn't hear of it. Although she was concerned about him, she couldn't worry over him. He wouldn't stand for it. They seemed to be developing a good working relationship and if she fretted over him, that would be ruined. On the other hand, she didn't want to risk Jared's wrath if Roberto overdid things and became ill. She sighed theatrically and blew her bangs out of her face. This job could turn out to be a true balancing act.

"In some ways, I felt that I never really knew him," Roberto Cruz said.

"That was probably because he was so much older than you."

"Yes." Roberto looked up and smiled. "Like all kids with big brothers who'd gone off to war, I idolized him."

They were working in the dining room again the next day and the older man was talking about his brother. Roberto had arrived in the middle of the morning. He'd been full of enthusiasm for the work and had started out with great energy. His energy had begun to flag, though, and Brittnie was ready to suggest a break.

She had been telling Roberto about the things she'd read in David's journal, though the cross-writing had hampered her progress and her eyes had begun to burn and blur after a few minutes.

"Anyone who volunteers to go off to fight a war they didn't start deserves to be idolized," Brittnie answered earnestly. She was searching rapidly through boxes of financial papers and old bills. As far as she could tell, they didn't have much value except perhaps as a bit of social history. Roberto had told her to dispose of them as she saw fit, so she would contact a friend at the historical society and see if they would be interested in preserving any of this. She clapped the lid on the box, scooted it aside and reached for another one.

Across from her at the table, Roberto did the same thing, standing to pull up the closed flaps of an old carton that had once held cans of beans. Immediately, he was wracked by sneezing and before he could recover and catch his breath, he began to wheeze.

Alarmed, Brittnie leaped to her feet and hurried

around the table, reaching for him. "Roberto, what can I do?"

"The...box," he said, pointing. "Some kind of flowers. I'm...ah...ah..." He sneezed. "Allergic," he finished on a gasp. His hand went to his throat as if trying to force in more air.

Brittnie grabbed the box and whipped it away from him. It contained flowers that had been dead for many years; the leaves, stems, and flower heads crumbling into dust that puffed out in a cloud when she jostled the carton. Quickly, she hurried it outside, set it on the back porch, then dashed back through the kitchen, grabbing a glass of water and a handful of damp paper towels along the way.

Roberto was slumped in his chair, fighting for breath. With frantic thoughts about his bad heart, Brittnie turned him slightly to make him more comfortable, loosened the top buttons on his polo shirt, then knelt beside him as she bathed his face which was an alarming shade of red. Urging his head forward, she gave him a drink of water. After a moment, he began to breathe more easily and he gave her a grateful look.

"Thanks, Brittnie, I think you probably saved my life." He tried to smile, but the attempt was ghastly. Sweat popped out to bead his forehead. Brittnie bathed his face again and chafed his hands hoping it would help his circulation.

She was on the verge of calling for emergency medical help when she heard a step behind her and Jared's voice say, "What the hell's going on here?"

Brittnie glanced over her shoulder as Jared stalked toward them. She stood, but before she could answer, he went on. "Is it his heart?"

"I don't know."

"Have you let him work too hard? He's only been here two days!" Jared nudged her aside, usurping her place beside Roberto.

Brittnie stumbled back, incensed that he would immediately think she was at fault when she was trying to do her best for his grandfather. She answered in a snappish tone. "No, I'm not working him too hard. He's a grown man. He works as hard as he wants to. For your information, he opened a carton that turned out to have old dried flowers in it. He started wheezing, and...."

"I should have known that something like this would happen." His tight-lipped expression and the stiff set of his shoulders testified to the anger he was holding in. Brittnie knew full well who he was angry with.

Roberto held up his hand. His color was rapidly improving and his breathing was calmer. "I'm all right, Jared. Don't fuss, and don't blame Brittnie." He straightened. "*I'm* the one who should have known what would happen. With all this other junk, of course David would have saved a box of old weeds." He tried an attempt at a smile. "Do you think he tried booby-trapping this place so we couldn't clean out his stuff?"

Brittnie returned his smile though she felt shaky. Her heart was just beginning to settle back from the place where it had jumped in her throat after her fright. She glanced at Jared. He was frowning at Roberto, but glanced up and transferred the frown to her.

"Roberto, why don't you go in the living room and lie down on the sofa?" she suggested, then glanced at her watch. "I'll fix some lunch."

"I don't want to put you to any trouble," Roberto protested.

"You're not. I was ready to eat anyway. So why don't

you join me?'' Jared could join them if he chose, but she was irritated with him so she really didn't care.

Roberto nodded. "I would feel better if I ate something."

He stood and leaned on the arm that Jared offered. She started to support him on the other side, but Jared gave her a look that had her dropping her hands to her sides and stepping back. As the two men moved toward the entry hall and the living room beyond, Brittnie turned toward the kitchen.

Jared seemed determined to make her responsible for his grandfather's health. It was completely unfair. She had told him she would watch out for Roberto, but she shouldn't be held fully responsible for the older man. Even Roberto had told him that. The more she thought about it as she pulled salad ingredients from the refrigerator and slammed them onto the counter, the angrier she became. Hurting Roberto was the last thing she wanted to do, and Jared should understand that.

She ripped apart a head of lettuce, dropped it into a bowl, and began tearing it into little pieces. She was going to tell Jared all of this as soon as they were out of Roberto's hearing. Employer or not, he couldn't blame her for what wasn't her responsibility.

When she heard the kitchen door open behind her, she glanced over her shoulder at Jared. She turned to face him, but before she could tell him what was on her mind, he said, "Couldn't you have stopped him?"

"From what?" she demanded, throwing her hands in the air. "Opening a box that looked perfectly innocent?"

"I asked you to watch out for him." Jared paced across the kitchen to face her.

"No, you *ordered* me to."

"And you can't follow orders?"

A haze of red washed before her eyes. "I *have been* watching out for him, but I don't see how you could have expected me to know what was inside that box!" Brittnie slapped her hands onto her hips and glared at him.

"I *expect* you to do your job."

"I am!"

They were at an impasse. Both of them holding their ground, refusing to back down. Tension crackled in the air between them.

Jared broke away first as if the anger rocketing through him forced him into action. He curled his fists at his sides. Brittnie wondered if he was trying to keep himself from wrapping them around her throat.

He took a couple of agitated turns around the room. "He won't quit," Jared said in a voice full of frustration. "He just won't quit."

"And you can't make him quit. Neither can I."

Jared cast her a dark glance, but she didn't back down. "I don't want to lose him." He ran a hand through his dark hair, which Brittnie thought showed the level of his distress. She'd never seen his hair disarranged, but now it fell away from his fingers in soft waves. She curled her own hands at her sides to keep from reaching up and brushing it back into place, then wondered if she was losing her mind to even consider such a thing when she was so furious with him.

He punched a finger toward her. "And don't give me that talk about how he's lived a long and productive life."

"I wouldn't dream of it," she gasped. "It hurts to lose someone you love no matter what their age."

At the horrified tone in her voice, Jared paused. Some of his anger and agitation seemed to level out. He ran his hand through his hair again and his angular face worked with emotion.

"The truth is, I've never lost anyone close to me."

"Your uncle…?"

"I really didn't know him well. He was something of a recluse, as I'm sure you've guessed. We saw him, but not often. Even Granddad didn't see him much."

"That's sad," she said sympathetically. "But you can't change him and you can't change what's going to happen to him…to all of us someday."

Jared's piercing gaze met hers. "You're thinking about your father."

Brittnie gave him a quick, startled glance, then she recalled that he had researched her just as she had him. "Yes. I am," she said. "He died of cancer. Three years ago."

She took a deep breath, momentarily letting the pain seep through her. It still hurt. It always would. She and Hal Kelleher had been very close.

"I'm sorry," Jared said. His tone was sincere and she bobbed her chin in acknowledgment. She knew he was only expressing regret over her father's death, not remorse for accusing her of being careless with Roberto's well-being. She was still hurt and incensed, but she felt empathy for him seeping in. She didn't welcome it, but she understood the frustration and helplessness that made him lash out. She'd felt the same way when her dad was diagnosed with the disease that took his life.

She turned away, opened some cans of soup, and poured them into a pan and set it on the stove. David Cruz's kitchen didn't run to anything as modern as a microwave oven, so she was quickly relearning how to cook and reheat food the old-fashioned way.

Brittnie adjusted the burner, then turned from the

stove to see that Jared was leaning against the counter with his arms crossed over his chest and his troubled gaze on her. She doubted that he was even focusing on her, but she brushed her hand across her face in case she had picked up a smudge of dust from her morning's work.

"Is something wrong?" Jared asked, focusing on her face.

"No," she answered. With nothing to do, she wandered over to the sink and tucked her hands into her back pockets as she leaned against it and faced him again. She blinked when she saw that Jared had moved up right behind her.

"You've smeared dirt on your face," he said, picking up a towel that lay on the counter. She reached to take it from him, but he said, "I'll do it."

She recognized it as a somewhat feeble peace offering, but when he took her chin in his hand and turned her face to the light streaming in the window, a shock ran through her. Her eyes flew to his face, but he was concentrating on his task and didn't meet her gaze. Brittnie's heart kicked into high speed. She was sure he could feel it pounding against his fingertips.

Why was he doing this? she wondered in a haze as the warmth from his fingers stole through her skin and seemed to heat the very bone of her jaw. And why was she letting him do it? This was totally and completely unprofessional. Uncalled for. Unwanted. She knew this, but when she moved her chin in his grasp, it was toward his touch, and not away.

Eyes wide, lips open to shivering breaths, she voiced her question. "Why are you doing this?"

Finally he met her eyes. A speck of humor danced in their darkness. "Because your face is dirty. I don't know you well, but I don't think you're the kind of woman who wants to be seen with a dirty face."

His words finally broke the spell of his touch. She tugged her chin away and said, "No, you don't know me well or you would know I don't invite my employers to…to wash my face for me."

He seemed amused by her response. "Let's say it's a payback."

"Whatever for?"

"You take care of my granddad—or at least you're supposed to. I was just taking care of you."

Something was going on here that she *really* didn't understand. Brittnie waved her hand dismissively. "There's no need. I'm just doing my job."

He lifted an eyebrow at her. Somehow he could do that with such flair, she thought grumpily. "And I was doing mine," he said.

Brittnie was trying to think of something to say when the soup boiled over in the pot. When it hissed and steamed its way onto the stove top, she whipped around, grabbed the towel, and moved it off the burner, grateful for the distraction. When she turned back, she saw that the door had opened and Roberto stood watching them, an intent, fixed expression on his face as he looked from her to his grandson.

A feeling of dread swept through her. She had the feeling something had happened while her back was turned and she wasn't going to like it when she found out what it was.

CHAPTER FIVE

"THAT boy works too hard."

Brittnie started and glanced up as Roberto entered the room after seeing Jared out the door. His face was creased in a ferocious frown. Jared had taken the remainder of the legal papers that pertained to his company, loading the cartons into his Jeep and saying he had to hurry back to work.

"He says the same thing about you."

"He worries too much about me," Roberto admitted. "And he doesn't need to. But in his case, I *do* need to worry. He works too hard and he doesn't get out enough."

"Oh? That's too bad," Brittnie murmured politely as she tried to hide her smile. The two men were so much alike, but they obviously didn't see it. She had decided they both worked too hard. She couldn't confirm Roberto's statement that Jared didn't get out enough. She'd seen him out with Linda Pomfort, but she certainly knew that Jared worked too hard and worried too much over his grandfather. The scene in the kitchen was proof of that. She still felt shaky from the storm of emotion he had created in her.

"He's a good boy. Well, a good man," Jared's proud grandfather amended. "Conscientious. His employees like him."

"I noticed that."

"You did? When?"

Brittnie busied herself with some loose items on the

78

dining table. "Oh, when I had my job interview. Everyone seemed to know they could come to him with a problem. He was…" She tilted her head thoughtfully. "Approachable," she concluded, and hoped it didn't sound too much like she'd been spending time daydreaming about him.

"You thought so? Approachable. I like that."

Roberto sat down and contemplated the boxes they had already set aside to go through that afternoon. No doubt, he was remembering the episode of the dried flowers, because he was cautious as he flipped the lid open and reached in for a handful of file folders. Seeing that nothing dangerous was going to leap out at him, he set them on the table and began sorting through them as he continued. "He needs something to think about besides work."

When he paused, Brittnie answered, "No doubt," in a distracted manner. The carton she'd just opened was full of bound ledgers. She felt guilty for not listening more closely to what Roberto was saying, but this was just too interesting to ignore.

As Roberto talked, she made occasional comments. She opened one of the ledgers and discovered that it was a financial record of David Cruz's law practice. Smiling slightly, she read copies of receipts for goods he had received in exchange for his legal services, including some live poultry and a whole hog.

"In fact, it's time for him to settle down and get married."

"Probably the best thing that could happen to him," Brittnie answered automatically. Her eyes widened as she read the ledger page. David had once received a Tiffany lamp as payment. She wondered where it was today. It could be worth a fortune. Not that the Cruz family seemed to need the money, but the lamp might be a nice sentimental keepsake for Roberto. Like his brother's war journals. She hadn't deciphered much so far because of the difficulty of reading the cross-writing, but what she'd seen made her heart ache—a young boy away from home for the first time, eating unfamiliar food and experiencing things much harsher than anything he'd known on his parents' Colorado farm.

"You agree, then?"

Brittnie started and had to take a moment to refocus on what they'd been discussing. "Certainly," she said heartily, hoping her answer would be a proper response. "There's no doubt about that."

"The problem is he doesn't know *what* he wants," Roberto said in a sour tone. He stood and dumped the papers from the file folders into a large box they had designated for recycling. When she looked up curiously, he said, "Old computer printouts from ten years ago. Nothing important."

Brittnie closed the account book she'd been reading and handed it to him. "I think you'll be interested in this. Best of all, it's easy to read."

He took it and flipped it open, then glanced up. "So you think Jared should get married?"

Brittnie stared. "I do?"

"That's what you just said."

Darn! Why hadn't she been paying attention? "I did?"

"In fact, the more I get to know you, the more I think he needs a woman just like you."

Her hand flew to her throat. Good grief! What *had* he been talking about? "He does?" she gasped. "I mean, no, he doesn't. I mean, he should marry someone he…he loves."

"Piffel," Roberto said, waving that idea away as if it was a drift of fog. "He needs to find someone like you who'll stand up to him. You two can always fall in love later."

Brittnie was too stunned to even try correcting that shaky logic. "Roberto, you've got to be kidding. In the space of one breath you went from saying he needs to find someone 'like' me to saying he and I can fall in love later. No. That's not...."

"It's a fine idea." He nodded slowly, smugly, as if he'd solved a tremendous problem. "I don't know why I didn't think of it sooner."

Because it's crazy? Brittnie almost blurted. Instead, she cast around for a minute, then said in a placating tone, "Roberto, I appreciate the thought that your grandson needs someone who is...like me...."

"Not *like* you," he insisted. "You."

"But," she trudged ahead. "That's not possible. He's my boss, and...."

"More piffel. Nobody cares about that kind of thing anymore."

"*I* do."

"Then, obviously, you need to develop a new way of thinking. He needs a woman in his life."

Brittnie almost mentioned Linda Pomfort, but it would just pull her deeper into a discussion she was trying to end. With a bright smile, she said, "Maybe we could talk about this some other time. Right now we have lots of work to do."

Roberto barked with laughter. "Scared you, did I? Well, never mind. It'll work out. My son and daughter-in-law are going to be in town this weekend. We're having a get-together at my house. It's her birthday. He's a doctor, you know. Has a practice in Phoenix."

"Who? Your son?" Trying to keep up with this sudden change of topic, Brittnie stammered, "Uh, no, I didn't know that."

"Moved down there a few years ago so Jared's mother could be in a warmer climate. What they got was hotter-than-hell, but they're happy."

"That's good."

"So you'll come?"

"Come where?" Brittnie shook her head. In a minute, she feared her ears would start ringing from the effort of following this conversation.

"To the party at my house. Lots of friends there. You'll like it."

"Oh, really," she demurred. "I can't, but thank you for inviting me."

Roberto had been leafing through the ledger as he talked. He stuck his finger in it and looked up. "Are you saying that you've got another date?"

"Well, no," she admitted. Unless she counted an evening spent with David Cruz's war journals.

"Then you must have so many friends you couldn't use a few more."

"I didn't say that," she said, frustrated.

"Then you'll be there," he answered decisively.

She couldn't think of any further arguments. "Yes, sir," she said, earning a grin from him. Shaking her head in admiration, she said, "It's really clever the way you get your own way like that."

"I've been practicing for many years." His eyes twinkled at her. "Jared's learning it, too, but I think the right woman could steer him in a better direction before he becomes too set in his ways. See, my problem was that I was widowed too young." He paused and his face softened. "Far too young," he said in a quiet tone, and with such longing in his face, that tears started suddenly to Brittnie's eyes.

Brittnie blinked them away and dredged up a bright tone. "Well, let's hope he finds her soon."

"Oh, he has," Roberto chuckled. "He has."

Brittnie didn't *at all* like his tone or the look he gave her when he said it.

"How do you get yourself into these things?" Shannon propped her elbow on the kitchen table, rested her chin on her palm and regarded her younger sister with fascination. Her deep blue eyes sparkled.

Brittnie gave her a disgruntled look. "This wasn't my fault," she insisted as she carried two soft drink cans to the table and handed one to Shannon. She sat down, popped the top of her soda can and said, "Roberto thought this up on his own."

"What are you going to do about it?"

"Ignore it and hope it goes away?" she suggested wistfully. "Jared has someone he's obviously interested in and, well, *I'm* certainly not going to pursue him."

"The girl he's interested in," Shannon said, thoughtfully. "The one we saw him with when we were out with Ben and Timmy."

"Yes? What about her?"

"I knew I'd seen her before but I couldn't place her. Then I remembered she was at Colorado State while I was there, though I didn't know her. We didn't exactly run in the same social circles."

Brittnie nodded. Shannon's education had been as hard-won as her own. Between work and school, she'd had little time for a social life of any kind. She'd turned down so many dates because of her work schedule that one potential suitor had nicknamed her "Can't Date Kelleher."

"Anyway," Shannon went on. "What I knew of her actually made me feel sorry for her."

"Why?"

"A case of poor-little-rich-girl. Her family had lots of money, but not much time for her. She usually spent school holidays with friends." Shannon paused. "It was sad. I heard somewhere that she'd been quite sick last year."

"That's too bad," Brittnie said, trying to connect the image of the neglected girl with the disdainful one who had talked to her about "knowing her bounds."

Shannon sipped her soda and changed the subject. "Sounds like you're going to get a close-up of the rich and famous of this town at Mr. Cruz's tomorrow night."

Brittnie grimaced. "I know."

"You don't have to sound like you're heading over to turn yourself in at a torture chamber. It'll be fun." She stood suddenly and strode toward the stairs. "Come on, let's go choose something for you to wear."

Fun, Brittnie thought nervously as she trudged along behind her sister. Fun as long as Roberto didn't start voicing his newest idea out loud.

Brittnie was pleasantly surprised when she saw Roberto's house. She knew that he, and Jared, were wealthy so she had expected an estate. What she found after she had spent half an hour searching for the place, was a charming little house that looked as though it had started out as someone's cabin, been upgraded, and made into a real home. It was close enough to the golf course that Roberto could play frequently. The house was surrounded by trees. In front of the house, and along the sweeping, curved drive were big beds full of bright fall flowers.

When she parked behind the other cars and glanced around, she saw why he'd bought the property in the first place. The view and the privacy were spectacular.

Reluctantly, she turned from the beautiful vista and looked at the house. It intrigued her that one of the Cruz brothers had a mansion while the other had a cabin. She wondered what kind of home Jared had—probably an apartment or condo, someplace close to his office, no doubt.

As Brittnie started toward the front door, her steps slowed. She still wasn't sure how she'd let Roberto and Shannon talk her into this, especially after his conclusion that she would make Jared a good wife. She admitted that she found Jared attractive and intriguing, though sometimes infuriating, and he probably did need a wife, but it wasn't going to be her. She'd finally started on her career. She had things to do. Good grief, she was only twenty-five.

Marriage wasn't in her plans, she concluded as she reached the front of the house, and the only reason she had dreamed about wedding dresses last night was because she obviously needed to get her subconscious mind under control.

Giving up on that line of thought, Brittnie stood by the carved oak door and tugged down the hem of her blue silk bomber-style jacket. Even though she knew she looked good in a calf-length skirt, turquoise-studded belt, and pale blue silk shirt, she felt self-conscious. Usually, she dressed to please herself, but tonight, it had been Jared's face she'd imagined when she'd picked out the shirt that she knew complimented her hair and eyes. Even her hair wasn't in its normal free-flowing style, but carefully tucked into a French braid. Now she was afraid she looked too prim and proper.

"Oh, the heck with it," she muttered as she rang the doorbell. She didn't know why she cared how she looked. She wasn't there to win approval, only to fulfill a promise to Roberto.

The door was answered by a middle-aged man who looked her over and smiled quickly. That smile, and the tilt of his head told her he was Jared's father, Roberto's son.

He ushered her inside. "Welcome. You must be Brittnie Kelleher. Dad said you were coming and everyone else he invited is here. I'm John Cruz."

Brittnie greeted him as he took her into the living room. She found herself in a space that ran the length of the house. At the end were huge plate-glass windows and a sliding door that led to a redwood deck. A kitchen and dining area were on her left and on the right were stairs that went up to a railed balcony which circled the top of the wall and gave access to the bedrooms. It was airy and modern, and exactly the opposite of David's house.

She admired the open floor plan even as her gaze flew up and around the room, noting the number of people that were there. Relieved, she saw that the room was crowded. It was much easier to mingle in a big crowd— and much easier to leave early if she felt uncomfortable, though she didn't know how that would happen considering the warmth with which she was greeted. John Cruz introduced her to his wife, Miranda, a petite woman with hair as dark as Jared's and lively gray eyes. John brought her the soft drink she requested, and Roberto swept up to greet her.

The four of them discussed the work in David's house.

Roberto urged Brittnie to tell what she had learned from David's journals and she found herself with a captive audience.

Even as she spoke, though, Brittnie couldn't keep her gaze from straying, wandering the room until she saw Jared enter from the deck beyond the glass sliding doors. When he walked in and his eyes met hers, Brittnie had the quirky thought that he'd been waiting for her. His gaze swept over her, noting the Southwestern cut of her clothing and her French-braided hair. When his mouth curved in a slight smile, Brittnie felt her heart whoosh down to her toes, then bobble up again.

As Jared made his way across the room, Brittnie felt warmth, unbidden and unwanted spread through her. She would like to think that it was because of the heat, but in fact, the room was cool, or that her drink was warm, but the glass of cola John had given her was full of ice. No, the heat was generated by being in the same room with Jared. She had noticed it before, especially the day he'd held her jaw and cleaned the dust from her face, but this time it hit her with the punch of a solar flare.

Confused and appalled, she glanced down. After all, he was dating another woman. Though Brittnie didn't see Linda here tonight, it was obvious that she meant a great deal to him. And, as she had told Roberto, Jared was her boss, not someone in whom she should have a romantic interest. Brittnie knew she had no right to feel such intense attraction to him. If only she could convince her body of what her mind already knew.

When Jared reached them, Brittnie looked up again, carefully forming a warm smile that she hoped hid the true chaos of her emotions.

"Hello, Brittnie," Jared said when he reached them. "Granddad said you were coming."

Brittnie couldn't tell from his tone of voice whether he approved or not. "Yes, well, it seemed to be important to him."

Roberto broke in impatiently, "Of course it is. She belongs here." To his family, he said, "Brittnie was just telling us about some of the things she's discovered in David's war journals. Go on, Brittnie," he urged.

Brittnie smiled, aware now that for all his talk about Jared needing to marry her, or someone like her, he'd invited her to this get-together so she could tell what she'd learned from David's journals.

Brittnie told about David's adjustment to boot camp and his second thoughts after joining the Canadian forces, and of his ultimate determination to stay and fight. She admitted that reading the journals was so difficult she could only manage a little at a time. Then the group broke up, with Roberto, John, and Miranda drawn away to enjoy their other guests.

Left alone with Jared, Brittnie took a careful sip of her cola and said, "Nice party."

Jared glanced around. "Yes. My parents have lots of friends. Granddad throws one of these whenever they come to town."

Silence stretched between them. Having exhausted that topic, Brittnie didn't know what to say. She felt awkward, remembering their last meeting, and her subsequent conversation with Roberto. Grumpily, she thought that this situation would be so much easier if she didn't find Jared so compelling. Even now, wearing an open-collared cotton shirt and a dark brown jacket of nubby silk, he looked far too good for her peace of mind. And she knew she *had* to stop thinking like that. Her lips tightened in irritation with herself.

"What's the matter?" he asked. "Hungry? Come on,

let's get some food. Granddad always has these things catered and he only buys the best.'' Taking her arm, he steered her toward the buffet table. He picked up a plate and handed it to her, then took one for himself.

Brittnie hung back and glanced around. ''You're not with a...date tonight?''

''You mean Linda?'' He shook his head, but his dark eyes were troubled. ''She...couldn't make it. Besides, as of last week, she's on some kind of rice and bean sprout diet.'' He glanced at the cheese and sauce-laden dishes. ''These are supposed to be low-fat, for the sake of Granddad's heart, but I don't think they'd be low enough for Linda.''

Brittnie couldn't think of anything to say to that except, ''Oh.'' She moved down the buffet table, putting small dabs of food on her plate.

''Oh, for cryin' out loud,'' Jared muttered, eyeing her plate in disgust. ''You're going to need a magnifying glass to locate the food on your plate.'' He took it away from her. ''I know you're hungry. So eat.'' He began piling on mounds of food.

Always aware of her appetite and the embarrassments it had caused her in the past, Brittnie stared at him in dismay.

''Don't worry,'' he said, a teasing glint crackling in his eyes. ''If anyone says anything, I'll tell them you're eating for two.''

''Don't you dare,'' she burst out, and he laughed, the rich sound lifting above the chatter around them. Roberto stood several feet away. Brittnie saw his head come up. He gazed at them for a few seconds, then gave a nod of approval.

She answered with a stern look that Jared intercepted.

"Why are you giving my grandfather the evil eye? I thought you liked him."

"I do like him. I just don't like some of his ideas."

Jared lifted an eyebrow at her as he took the plate he'd filled for her and headed for the deck. A cool wind was blowing, but he pulled a glass and wrought-iron table and two chairs into a sheltered corner. He grabbed a lit candle from another table and placed it between them. It cast an intimate glow that was belied by the no-nonsense tone in Jared's voice. "You don't like his ideas about the job you're doing?"

"It's not that." She waved her fingers dismissively. "It's nothing."

Jared gazed at her as though he wanted further explanation, but Brittnie lifted her brows as he did so often, and gave him a steady look that told him she wouldn't answer any more questions about it.

His lips twitched as if he knew what she was telling him.

"Eat," he said, after a minute, picking up his own fork and digging in. She knew he would probably ask her again because everything to do with Roberto concerned him, but she was also learning that she could hold her own with him. That knowledge brought its own undercurrent of excitement which Brittnie wasn't prepared to examine too closely.

She knew she should. There was no doubt that she should give careful thought to the feelings she was developing for this man. She should try to determine why she sometimes felt as if light was flooding through her when she saw him, and why at other times, she experienced total exasperation.

Instead, she turned her attention to her plate which Jared had loaded with smoked salmon, roast beef, and several kinds of salads. She took a small bite of the salmon. She didn't usually care for smoked salmon, but this one had a delicate taste. She closed her eyes, letting it sit on her tongue, then she chewed slowly, concentrating on the flavor as she tried to identify it.

"Not hickory," she murmured. "Mesquite."

She opened her eyes to see that Jared had paused with his fork halfway to his mouth, holding it, apparently forgotten, in his fingers. His eyes were fixed on her, the lids hooded in a mysterious and yet compelling way.

Brittnie's throat tightened in reaction. "What is it, Jared?"

He swallowed, though she didn't think he'd had any food in his mouth, set his fork down, looked away, cleared his throat, then looked back at her. "Hell, Brittnie, eating with you is...."

She leaned forward, waiting for him to finish.

"...An adventure."

Disconcerted, she sat back and folded her hands in her lap. "You're the one who marched me over here with...."

"That's not what I mean." He sighed and stroked his chin. "You just seem to enjoy things so much."

She was taken aback. "Excuse me? That's bad?"

"I didn't say it was bad," he answered, irritation edging his voice. "It's different."

"Different than...?"

"The women I know. Most of the time they don't eat much in front of the men they date. They must think it's not politically correct or something."

Brittnie felt a smile forming. "I think you've already figured out that with me, what you see is what you get. I'm curious about things. I like learning new things, new information, which is one reason I became a librarian. I enjoy life," she said, slicing off another thin piece of salmon. "I like food. I don't mind getting messy when I'm working." She ate the salmon, then lifted her glass and glanced at him over the rim. "And besides, this isn't a date."

His eyes narrowed, but he lifted his own glass in a salute as he answered, "As you say, this isn't a date."

In spite of that, when they returned to their food, Brittnie began to sense an awareness between them that grew as the seconds ticked by. Now that he had commented on her enjoyment of things, she was even more aware of them herself. She took pleasure in tasting each of the delicious portions he'd put on her plate, and she couldn't help watching him, thinking that her enjoyment had affected him, too.

The sunlight faded behind the surrounding mountains. The only light between them was the candle he'd placed on the table. Even the light from Roberto's living room barely reached the corner where they sat.

Brittnie gave a fleeting thought to how it must look with the two of them in such an intimate setting, away from everyone else, but the thought didn't linger. She was enjoying herself too much.

Before they finished, Roberto came out to join them. "A beautiful view, isn't it?"

Startled, Brittnie turned around. She hadn't even noticed exactly when the sun had disappeared. The lights of nearby homes twinkled through the trees like fireflies tucked into black velvet. "Um, yes, it is," she agreed.

Roberto gave her another of the smug smiles she was coming to know and dread. He turned away before she could say anything. "Why don't you two come inside now?" he asked as he opened the door. "It's time for

Miranda's birthday cake and she's going to open her gifts.''

Brittnie looked at Jared in alarm.

He shook his head. "Don't worry about it. You're a guest. My mother certainly wouldn't expect a gift from you."

He held Brittnie's chair and she stood, shaken to realize he'd known what she was thinking. The entire evening was taking on a surreal quality, as if she'd landed somehow in a dream. She was in a roomful of strangers, yet she didn't feel out of place. She was with a man she barely knew in some ways, but seemed to understand on a very basic level—and even more surprising, he seemed to understand her. When she felt his hand at the back of her waist, she shivered. She even seemed to know his touch.

She longed to get away from here, to have some distance and gain some perspective, but that was impossible just now.

"Come on. Granddad likes an audience when he does this."

Inside, the guests were gathered around the dining table which had been cleared by the caterers.

A large cake, frosted in creamy white frosting and decorated with bright orange nasturtiums sat in the center of the table. John lit one candle in the center of the cake, Miranda blew it out, and everyone clapped as they kissed and he handed her a small, flat box. From it she pulled a narrow diamond bracelet and she kissed him again.

Roberto made a little speech about how special Miranda was to the family, especially since she'd been willing to take on John and put up with him for so many

years, which drew laughs from the crowd and a mock
frown from John.

Brittnie smiled, recalling family birthdays at home.
There had never been anything as beautiful or expensive
as that bracelet, or perfect as this cake. In fact, for several years, she and Shannon had baked their father's
cake. It had invariably been lopsided and topped with
runny frosting, but he'd declared it delicious. They had
finally mastered the art of cake baking for the last birthday he'd celebrated before his death. Unbidden, tears
started to her eyes.

Jared, who had been standing beside her, looked down
suddenly, as if she'd called his name, though she knew
she hadn't made a sound. "Brittnie? What's wrong?"

Feeling foolish, she shook her head and cleared her
throat. "Nothing. This is lovely."

He didn't say a word, but reaching between them, he
took her hand and clasped it in his.

Brittnie's throat clogged with even more tears because
he was comforting her and didn't even know why she
was crying. She hadn't thought he would be a sensitive
man. Her breathing was ragged for a moment, then
steadied. When he felt her relax, Jared squeezed her
hand and released it. Brittnie thanked him with a shaky
smile.

Jared looked at her with sympathy and awareness in
his eyes, but it was tinged with uncertainty, as if he
didn't know quite what to think of her, or of his reactions
to her.

That made two of them, Brittnie thought with an inward sigh. This whole thing was way out of her experience.

Miranda opened the remainder of her gifts while the
caterers began serving the cake. In a moment, Roberto

was standing before them with two dessert plates in his hands.

Jared took one and handed the other to Brittnie as his grandfather looked them over, his eyes full of expectations.

Brittnie took a bite of the cake, which melted on her tongue. She took another tiny bite and chewed slowly to savor it.

"Did you hear what I said about your mom, Jared?"

"Yes, Granddad." Jared's eyes were on Brittnie as she swallowed the bite she'd taken and cut off another tiny bit. "I know you've always liked mom."

"She's the best thing that ever happened to John. She's smart and strong."

"I know that. Why are you telling me?"

"Because you need to marry someone like your mother."

"I do?" Amusement was clear in his voice as he exchanged a look with Brittnie, but his smile faded when he saw her stricken face.

Brittnie's fork clattered against her plate. "Roberto," she croaked in a pleading tone. The cake had turned to sawdust in her throat. "Don't. Really, you shouldn't."

He ignored her and forged ahead. "Brittnie's personality is a lot like your mother's. She stands up to you. You ought to marry her. In fact, I think a Thanksgiving wedding would be just about perfect."

CHAPTER SIX

"OH, ROBERTO," Brittnie moaned as she closed her eyes, instantly and completely embarrassed. She squinted at him, wincing in anticipation of the expression on Jared's face, though she didn't dare look at him. It was bad enough just imagining the way he must be glaring at her. "Why did you have to say that?"

"Because it's true," the older man responded with a shrug.

"Granddad," Jared said in a voice that was one breath away from being a menacing growl. "I don't need you to tell me who to marry."

Brittnie finally chanced a look at him. His mouth was tight and his complexion had turned a dusky red. His eyes snapped to her, and then away. She took a half step back. Not that she hadn't expected his reaction, but surely he didn't think *she* had anything to do with this, that she had planted this crazy idea in Roberto's head?

"Somebody needs to. You're getting nowhere on your own." Roberto thrust his chin out.

Brittnie started to turn away as she said shakily, "I'm sure you two want to talk about this alone, so I'll...."

Jared's hand shot out to grasp her wrist and bring her up short. "You're not going anywhere. This concerns you, too." He released her, but the force of his statement, and her own surprise kept her in place. "In fact, it probably concerns you more than it does me."

He *did* think she had something to do with Roberto's appalling idea. Straightening, she gave him a steady glare from eyes that snapped with silver fire. He didn't even seem to notice because he was focused on his grandfather. His own eyes had grown so dark the pupils seemed to have disappeared completely. The expression on his face was one of stubborn anger. Roberto's was exactly the same, but his color was rising.

Alarmed, Brittnie stepped between the two men. "Roberto, your heart. Don't get yourself upset."

"I won't," he responded with dignity. "If he'll take my suggestion."

"Suggestion?" Jared choked out, staring at Roberto in amazement. "That was more than a suggestion."

"All right, then, call it a very *strong* suggestion, but it's something you should think about." Roberto held up his hands. "I know what's going through your head."

"You couldn't possibly," Jared said between his teeth.

"You think you're going to marry Linda."

Jared's hand shot out in a tight little gesture. "*Linda* thinks I'm going to marry Linda."

Brittnie swallowed a gasp. Both men glanced at her, then went back to their argument. She gulped a couple of more times to tamp down the surge of disappointment that filled her. She didn't know why she was surprised, she'd suspected it all along. And besides, it was none of her business, something else she'd been telling herself all along. Still, she couldn't help the surge of dismay that engulfed her.

"You've talked to her about it, then?" Roberto's eyes narrowed shrewdly. "Or has she been the one doing the talking?"

"It doesn't matter which of us...."

"No, it doesn't," Roberto broke in dismissively, waving his hand as if it truly mattered no more than morning fog. "It would never work. You two have known each other too well and too long to get married now. Jared, your personality is so strong, you'd walk all over her, and she would let you get away with it. You'd stay at that office working day and night, never be home. She wouldn't see you, but she wouldn't complain. She'd be miserable, but she'd stick it out because it means security for her. She's become too dependent on you, and you've let her do it."

Tension snapped in the air between the two men. A muscle jumped in Jared's jaw as he stared at his grandfather. "Thank you for your analysis of the situation, but it's not your business, Granddad."

Brittnie felt sorry for Jared. It must be intensely embarrassing to have someone he loved bring his private business out before a near stranger in a roomful of people. She started, suddenly recalling that they were in the middle of a party, glanced around. No one seemed to be paying the least bit of attention to them. Seeing that brought a bubble of hysterical laughter to her throat. The two men before her were showing all the belligerence and determination of a couple of gunslingers at a showdown. She couldn't believe no one else was noticing.

Roberto broke the tension between them by saying, "I know you feel responsible for Linda, but as long as you do, you're making her weak. It means she'll always depend on you and never get out on her own and settle on what she wants to do with her life."

While Brittnie was trying to absorb this quick, but thorough assessment of Jared's potential fiancée, Jared's face had become even harder.

"It's really none of your business, Grandfather."

"Humph, so you just said. How many times have I heard that in the past year?"

"Obviously not enough times for it to sink in yet," Jared answered. His voice was weary, but not unkind.

With a shake of his head, Roberto turned to Brittnie and took her hand in his. "I'm sorry I've embarrassed you, but you already knew I was thinking about this."

"Oh, Roberto," she said, her gray eyes swimming with humiliated tears. "Thinking about it and saying it are two different things."

"Well, matters have been drifting long enough." With a dignified nod, he moved back to his guests, leaving Brittnie and Jared standing alone.

"Wait here," Jared commanded. "I'll tell my parents we're leaving, then we have to talk."

They didn't have to do any such thing. While he was speaking to his parents, Brittnie whirled around and hurried out the door. She knew it was unforgivably rude not to tell her hosts goodbye, but she was too upset to worry about it. Perhaps she could make it right at some time in the future—if she survived the embarrassment of this night.

Because she didn't like the burden of dealing with a purse at a party, she'd left it locked in her car and carried her keys in the pocket of her denim skirt. She grabbed them out now, and with them in hand, rushed down the driveway to her car. When the night air hit her, she gulped it in, grateful for the cold on her burning face.

Brittnie couldn't even begin to sort out the mixture of mortification, anger, and dismay that charged through her in waves. She certainly understood Roberto's concern for Jared, but he'd had absolutely no right to say what he'd said! What's more, she was distraught to learn that Jared and Linda did intend to marry. Why should she care? It was none of her business, and yet, that was what disturbed her the most. Her heart was pounding, and her face was burning, but it wasn't because of the mad dash she was making to her car.

She called herself every kind of a fool because she had somehow allowed herself to have fantasies about Jared, to become attracted to him. They didn't know each other well and what he knew of her he didn't seem to like. He thrived on being in control of every situation; a workaholic; with a girlfriend she now knew was his fiancée. Brittnie *knew* all that, and still, she had entertained foolish notions.

Her own stupidity was even more distressing than Roberto's announcement to Jared.

She had almost reached her car when she heard footsteps behind her. Because she knew it was Jared, she didn't even turn around. Her long legs stretched out to a sprint as she made a desperate dash.

"Brittnie, wait. I want to talk to you."

She fell against the door, and, trembling with reaction, looked over her shoulder and shook her head at him, though she knew he couldn't see her in the dusk. She had her key in the car's lock by the time he reached her. Turning it, she grasped the handle and jerked the door open, spilling pale yellow light across them both. She spoke to him in a voice breathless with shock and anger. "No. I don't want to talk...."

"Did you have anything to do with Granddad's crazy idea?" Jared interrupted.

Eyes snapping fire, she turned a furious face to him. "Certainly not!"

"But you knew what he had in mind."

It was a statement, not a question, rapped out in a staccato tone of voice that infuriated her even more. She was so angry, in fact, that she could barely answer. "I knew."

"How long did you know?"

Furious, Brittnie slammed the car door shut and swung around to face him. She immediately knew she was at a disadvantage because she had shut off her source of light, but she was too incensed to care.

"For a few days, Mr. District Attorney," she snapped, insulted by his cross examination. "But I thought he was joking."

"This is no joke."

"No, it isn't."

"And you swear you didn't have anything to do with it?"

She threw her hands out, barely able to keep herself from slugging him. "How many ways do I have to say it? This was completely his own idea. *He's* the one hearing wedding bells. Not me."

He stared at her for a long moment. He took a breath. She took a breath. They looked at each other and seemed to run out of fury at the same time. They turned as one, and slumped against her car.

"Where does he come up with this stuff?" Jared asked the universe in general. He rubbed the heels of his hands against his eyes.

"He thinks he's got your best interests at heart."

"He's driving me insane," Jared moaned. "He never gives up his meddling. If it's not the business, it's my personal life. We used to be close. We worked well together, but since he retired...."

"You've been at odds."

"In a big way." He paused, then snorted in disgust. "I guess I should be grateful he didn't say I should marry you in front of all the guests."

"Or Linda. Your fiancée would have been hurt." Brittnie could sympathize with that. *She* was hurting.

Jared lifted one shoulder. "Well, maybe."

Brittnie turned her head and stared at him. Maybe? What kind of response was that? He didn't elaborate. Instead, he straightened away from the car and looked down at her. At that moment, the full moon peeked through obscuring clouds, so she could see his face.

"If we ignore this, it may go away."

"Excuse me?"

Jared propped his elbow on his hand, rubbed his chin and gave her a considering look from beneath his lashes. "Yeah. I think that's the secret to dealing with this."

"Ignoring what Roberto said?" she asked, doubtfully.

"It's the only way."

"Ignoring it doesn't sound to me like dealing with it."

"Oh, you'd be amazed at what I've learned to ignore from him." Jared's tone was so long-suffering, Brittnie had to fight the need to put her arm around him and give him a sympathetic squeeze—which she knew was a pretty good indication of how rattled she was by all this.

Instead, she edged away, sliding a few inches along the car's polished surface. No need to place herself in the path of temptation. Feeling sympathy for him could lead right back to all those silly notions that had shattered at her feet a few moments ago. She made an effort to bring herself back to the subject at hand. "Besides, you don't seem like the type to ignore something like this."

"I don't?" he asked. "What type do you think I am?"

"I *know* what type you are," she scoffed. "You're the take-charge, grab-the-bull-by-the-horns, get-things-done, set-things-right type."

Now he really looked at her, his dark eyes searching her face. "Not the, I-can-ignore-this type?"

"Absolutely not."

"So, in your opinion, we have to deal with this somehow?"

"Yes," she said, peering at him through the darkness.

"Okay," he agreed, far too easily. "How?"

She clapped her hands onto her hips. "I should think that would be obvious. You simply go to your grandfather, tell him you're going to marry Linda, and to mind his own business."

"I tried that already, remember?"

They stared at each other again, turned, and slumped once more against the side of her car.

"So we just ignore it?" she asked, digging at the gravel with the toe of her shoe. "Even if he brings it up again?"

"And I have no doubt he will," Jared said, resignation in his voice. "Even he says he's as persistent as a tick on a hound dog."

Brittnie snickered at the idea of such a statement coming from the refined Roberto Cruz and she saw the flash of Jared's teeth as he grinned, too.

"It'll be hard," Jared went on. "But don't you see, ignoring what he said is all we *can* do."

Brittnie crossed her arms at her waist. "I guess you're right. He's bound to drop it when he sees that we're totally uninterested in each other, except, of course on a professional, employer/employee basis."

"Without a doubt," Jared agreed.

"I mean, when he sees that we behave in only the most disinterested way, he'll forget about what he said."

"Sure," Jared agreed, but she didn't like the tone in

his voice. "And maybe he didn't notice how we ate dinner together on his deck."

She sighed. "I don't suppose we could convince him we were discussing the progress of my work?"

"Not after the soulful way you were looking at me."

Brittnie started. "Soulful? I never did any such thing. Besides, you're the one who dragged me out there, arranged the table, arranged the chairs, put a candle between us."

"I knew you'd need some light so you could see me to give me soulful looks."

Brittnie bit her lip, trying to hold back a laugh. "If I'd known you, and your grandfather, were going to get such bizarre ideas, I would have blown out the candle."

"And how would that have looked? Like we wanted to be alone in the dark, maybe?"

She couldn't argue with that, darn it! Instead, she straightened, dusted her hands together as if she was ridding herself of something, and said briskly, "We're straying from the point of our discussion. We've made a definite agreement to ignore your grandfather's idea that I'm the woman you should marry, right?"

"That's right."

"And that, in the future, we'll treat each other with only professional courtesy."

"If we can manage that," he agreed.

"Fine."

"Fine."

Brittnie nodded and turned, prepared to climb in her car and get the heck out of there before she did something crazy herself, like telling him she didn't mean a word she'd said, that she couldn't seem to think of him in a businesslike way, especially when she found him so compelling, intriguing, and downright sexy. She reached for the door where her keys still hung in the lock, but he was blocking the way.

"Excuse me," she said. "I need to go."

He didn't move away. Instead, he turned to her and said, "It's not as though we're attracted to each other."

Brittnie blinked. She couldn't tell if he was joking or not. "Uh-uh," she said, shaking her head.

"And just to prove it, we should try an experiment." His hand came up to cup her shoulder.

"An…experiment?" she asked, moving her shoulder tentatively to see if he would drop his hand. He didn't, and she wasn't sure she wanted him to. Her heart accelerated to a quick, light patter in her chest.

His other hand stole around her waist. Her heart nearly thumped its way through her ribs. "I think you're… interesting, Brittnie."

"Interesting?" Talk about damned with faint praise.

He drew her closer. "More than interesting. Make that intriguing."

"That's better," she approved. Her common sense screamed at her to push away from him, that this was yet another of the crazy ideas that seemed to be bouncing around tonight, but she didn't. She specifically told her arms to stay at her sides, to hang there, as limply as lead weights, but they didn't. Completely against her will, they moved up and around his neck.

"You see," Jared continued. "When I find something intriguing, I like to find out as much as possible about it."

"But strictly in a professional, totally detached way," she agreed solemnly, though her breath seemed to be having a hard time making its way out of her throat.

"Like an experiment," he agreed.

"Exactly what has intrigued you so much that you

want to find out about it in a professional, totally detached way?'' Brittnie asked.

In spite of the feeble moonlight, she could see Jared's lips quirk. ''Your mouth,'' he said.

''Oh,'' was all she had time to respond before that quirky smile of his met her lips. Oh, no, was all she had time to think as his taste and his warmth stole through her. Oh, this meant trouble, was her next thought, and then her thoughts flattened out and spiraled away completely. She concentrated only on feeling, on the sound of his breathing, the puff of his breath against her skin, the smoothness of his shaven jaw against her cheek.

His lips were so warm that they sent heat spreading through her in waves. The scent of his skin filled her, spicy with his aftershave, tangy with the sweet saltiness of his own essence. Her hands gripped his shoulders, hanging on as the world spun, righted itself, and then spun in the opposite direction.

This isn't what she had wanted. This certainly isn't what she had planned, but it was wonderful. She moved closer, dove her hands into the midnight thickness of his hair and held on as he kissed her over and over until her lips tingled and her breath was gone.

At last, he pulled away, as breathless as she was and said, ''What... What do you think?''

Think? She didn't know how. She'd abandoned that pointless activity five minutes ago. She blinked and her head bobbed as if the heat they had generated had softened the cords of her neck. ''About what?''

He chuckled and nuzzled her cheek with his nose, sending ripples of pleasure through her. ''That we can treat each other in a professional way, an employer/employee way, and not give my grandfather ideas about you being the kind of girl I should marry?''

"No…um, no problem," she answered, still trying to get her bearings. Darn, why did it feel as if his arms were the one place on earth she was supposed to be? She pulled away with great dignity and said, "What do you think?"

He shook his head as if he was trying to clear it. "You're right. No problem." He reached up and tugged at his collar. "Didn't feel a thing. Did you?"

"Not a thing." She leaned against the car so her knees wouldn't buckle, proving what a liar she was.

"Good. That's settled, then. I'll tell Linda."

"You'll tell Linda what?" she asked in a horrified tone. Good grief, how could she have forgotten about his fiancée? How could *he?*

He seemed to shiver in the darkness, shaking his arms as if he was trying to see if they still worked. "If by chance, Granddad's insane notion gets back to her, I'll tell her it's strictly his idea."

Pain stabbed through Brittnie's heart, but she nodded. A tiny part of her pointed out that she ought to feel used and abused by Jared because he'd kissed her like she was water and he was dying of thirst. Another part reminded her that she'd been a full participant in that kiss, too. "That…that sounds…fine."

"If she doesn't hear about Granddad's idea, I won't tell her a damned thing."

"That's probably best. So that your grandfather will leave us alone, when we see each other, we'll be disinterested, courteous, professional. If he says anything else like he did tonight, we'll ignore him."

"Yes, and I'll stop being the take-charge, take-the-bull-by-the-horns type."

She choked on her laughter.

"At least in this situation," he amended.

"Excellent plan." Sticking out her hand, she said, "Let's shake on it." The truth was, she was already shaking in reaction to his kiss, but he didn't need to know that. A take-charge kind of guy could really use information like that to his own advantage.

Jared took her hand, gave it a quick grasp, then dropped it. "I'll see you then, Brittnie." He was brisk and as businesslike as he'd promised to be.

"Good night, Jared," she answered in the same tone. He opened her car door for her, she slipped behind the wheel, and started the motor. Jared stepped back and she drove away, her head high. It wasn't until she made the turn at the bottom of the driveway, that she let the starch seep out of her spine.

She slowed the car and concentrated on the road as she tried to sort out what had just happened. She'd been a fool, that much was obvious, but she didn't have to repeat the experience. Holding to their agreement would be easy, she told herself.

As long as he never touched her again.

For the next week, Brittnie worked steadily. Too steadily. She started early in the morning and worked until she was ready to drop. One benefit was that she discovered the journals of Magdalena Cruz in a metal footlocker and set them aside for Roberto, but she was exhausting herself. If insomnia troubled her, and it did most nights, she worked then, too, usually on David Cruz's diaries. What drove her was the memory of her evening with Jared. It took her two days to recover from the kiss, and her own stupidity in submitting to it.

It took her another two days to reconcile herself to the knowledge that she had cooperated with it and enjoyed it.

For two more days, she was angry with Jared for kissing her when he was virtually engaged to marry someone else.

On the seventh day, she quit beating herself up over it and rested.

She had heard nothing further from Jared, which suited her just fine. At least that's what she told herself. She didn't need to spend time with him, or even thinking about him, especially now that she knew he and Linda truly intended to marry, in spite of what his grandfather might think.

She couldn't help wondering about what Roberto had said—that Linda had become too dependent on Jared. She knew they'd known each other for many years which certainly accounted for the closeness she'd seen between them. Brittnie admitted that she was no expert on this whole male/female thing and maybe she was reading the signs wrong, but the closeness of the two of them seemed to be that of friendship rather than love.

On the other hand, the lusty, breath-stealing, knee-melting kiss she and Jared had shared hadn't possessed a speck of friendship. There had been no love there, either, though. It had been the purest form of awareness, experimentation. Lust. They had both been fooling themselves when they'd said they should try it out, then ignore each other. It was going to be between them now as clearly as an elephant dancing on the tabletop. She was glad she hadn't seen him all week because she was having so much difficulty squaring that kiss with the honorable man she knew him to be.

Roberto didn't come to the house to work with her for a few days because Jared's parents were still visiting. When he returned, she felt awkward, still irritated with him for embarrassing her. She got past that in a few minutes because he asked immediately about David's journals and what more she had learned and she was eager to tell him. He listened to every word with rapt attention and she was struck once again by how desperately he wanted to know his brother.

"I can't imagine anything more horrible than the trench warfare he must have endured," Brittnie told him. "It was horrifying. Did he ever say exactly why he ran off to Canada to enlist? Dreams of battlefield glory, maybe?"

The two of them were in the kitchen preparing lunch. Brittnie had finished cataloging one box of books in the library and Roberto had been tagging items to be donated to the historical society.

"He never talked about it at all," Roberto answered, grating cheese and spreading it over tortillas for the quesadillas he was making.

Brittnie turned from the refrigerator with salad ingredients in her hands. "You mean he never talked about his reasons?"

"He never talked about anything connected with that war. Even when I signed up for the marines and went off to World War II, my big brother didn't give me a word of advice or help." Roberto didn't sound bitter. He shrugged. "Go back to telling me what you've read in his journals while I've been gone."

Obligingly, as they ate lunch, Brittnie spoke of the transformation that seemed to be taking place, changing the Colorado farm boy into a hardened veteran, of the things he'd endured. When she finished, Roberto shook his head. "It would have helped me if I'd known that," he said quietly. "I would have understood him better."

"Maybe it will be explained in the last journal," Brittnie responded, trying to comfort him. "But he must have written a great deal in that last one."

"What do you mean?"

"Up to now, he seems to have used up one journal every six months, but from what I can tell, there's a year of the war left, and there's only one more journal in the box. I think there should be two."

"Maybe he wrote less as the war was winding down."

"Perhaps," Brittnie agreed. "In the meantime, you've got your mother's journals to read. They should be fascinating."

"Yes," Roberto agreed. "And easier to read."

Brittnie smiled. The two of them finished lunch, did the dishes, and returned to work. It was late that evening that she finished the last of David's journals and discovered that there had to be one more. She knew he hadn't been discharged from the marines until months after the war was over because she'd found his discharge papers in her search. Disappointed, she told Roberto about it the next day.

"It has to be here somewhere," the older man insisted.

"Well, perhaps," Brittnie agreed.

"I'll find it," he said, an intent look in his eyes. "You do your other work and I'll look for it."

And look he did. While Brittnie carefully researched and cataloged the books in David's library, she could hear Roberto tearing through the house. He reopened boxes they had already gone through, searched shelves, drawers, bookcases, and cabinets. Brittnie forced him to take a break in midafternoon, but it didn't last long. He was back at the search in a few minutes. He kept it up all that day, then appeared in the library doorway, his usually immaculate clothing dirty and stained, his hair tousled and his face red.

Alarmed, Brittnie stood and rushed to him. "Roberto, why don't you just leave it for now? We'll come across that missing journal, I'm sure."

He shook his head. "I'll find it," he said stubbornly. "I'll find it."

"But at what risk to your health?" she demanded. "Roberto, surely that journal isn't worth killing yourself over...."

"You sound just like my grandson."

"Good!" Brittnie wagged her finger at him. "And if you don't behave, I'll call your grandson and he'll fix you but good!"

"I know my limitations."

"No, you don't." She saw that she was only making him more recalcitrant so she forced herself to calm down. She took a steadying breath and tried for a teasing tone. "I'm a rancher's daughter, remember? I can rope and tie you if I have to."

He didn't respond to the forced lightness in her tone. "I know what I'm doing. This is important to me."

"And your good health is important to *me*," she said. "And to your family."

Roberto turned away. "I'll see you tomorrow."

Brittnie watched him leave, his steps slow and tired. No matter what he said, he didn't know his limitations.

Brittnie was relieved that evening when Shannon dropped by, bringing food, including a German chocolate cake their mother had sent. Brittnie cut big slices for them and they sat at the kitchen table savoring their dessert as Brittnie talked about her worries regarding Roberto.

"You're going to have to call Jared and get him to help you," Shannon said.

"I know that. I told Roberto that, too, but I don't want to do it. Jared already thinks I'm not taking care of him."

Ever the loyal sister, Shannon said, "It's not right that he puts that burden on you. But it sounds like there are things, serious things, going on between the two of them.''

"And I'm involved whether I want to be or not.''

"So you're going to have to ask Jared for help.''

Brittnie nodded and thoughtfully chewed a bite of cake. She knew that, but she didn't want to do it. It would be like admitting she couldn't do her job.

Though she tried to slow him down, Roberto was back at his search the next day, this time, exploring the attic. Brittnie carried out her threat and called Jared, but he was in Silverton for the day. Sandra promised to get a message to him. While waiting for him to call, Brittnie became absorbed in her work. She didn't realize how much time had passed, or that the house was unusually quiet until late in the morning.

Worried, she hurried upstairs to the second floor, gave it a quick search, then went on to the attic. She found Roberto sitting in an old wing chair. At first, she thought he'd found the journal because his hands seemed to be holding something before him. When she approached, though, she saw that his hands were empty, resting loosely in his lap. Her eyes shot to his face, where huge sweat beads stood out on his forehead. He turned his head and his eyes rolled her way.

"Roberto, what is it?'' she asked, kneeling before him and taking his clammy hands in hers.

"Better call the doctor, honey. I've done what everyone told me not to do and, my heart....''

Brittnie scrambled to her feet and raced for the phone.

CHAPTER SEVEN

"WHAT happened?"

Brittnie had known this was coming. She had known Jared would be here because she had phoned his office and left an urgent message with his assistant right after she had called for an ambulance. In the waiting area of the emergency room, she paced, then sat, then paced again while Roberto was being examined.

She was back to sitting on the hard vinyl sofa, leaning over at the waist, resting her face in her hands. Her mind continually replayed the moment she had found him, the struggle the paramedics had getting him down the stairs, the ride in the ambulance to the hospital where Roberto, pale and gasping, had been whisked away.

The situation was different, but she couldn't seem to separate the images from those of her father's death. Though his illness had been long, and his death expected, her sense of helplessness was the same.

When the door had burst open and rapid steps crossed the room, she had known it was Jared without lifting her head. She did so now, taking a breath and bracing herself for the onslaught of questions—and accusations—that he would throw at her.

Slowly, her head came up. His hair was disheveled as if he'd been running his hands through it in agitation and his face was strained. As expected, his eyes snapped with fury. "I thought you were supposed to be watching him."

"I was." She stood, automatically taking up a defensive stance with her shoulders squared as she faced him.

"You're getting paid to watch him." The staccato tone of his voice made her want to snap back at him. She knew he was frightened, but that didn't make his accusations any easier to bear.

"I did...."

"Not closely enough. What happened? Did you get your nose buried in a book and forget there was an old man with a bad heart upstairs?"

Because that was so close to the truth it stung, Brittnie lashed back at him. "And where were you if you were so concerned? When I saw he was overdoing it and I couldn't get him to stop, I tried to call you, but you were gone. Sandra couldn't even contact you. Did you have an important lunch date?"

His brown eyes crackled with fire as he marched up to face her. They were standing almost toe to toe. She could literally feel the heat of his anger blasting over her. "I was in a meeting. Not that it's relevant. We're talking about your neglect of your duties."

Speechless with fury, she glared at him. "*My* neglect? I did what I could, but you of all people know Roberto won't listen, only does what he feels like doing. You're being completely unfair."

"It's unfair to ask you to do your job?"

"Ooooh!" Throwing her hands in the air, she whirled away. "You're stubborn. Bullheaded and stubborn. It runs in your family. It *gallops* through your family!" She stomped over to a window that faced the parking lot. Tears of anger and frustration as well as ones of fury with Jared spurted into her eyes. She refused to give him the satisfaction of seeing her cry so she tilted her head back and squeezed her eyes shut, forcing the tears away. She breathed in, slowly and carefully, to calm herself.

Once she had a measure of control, she asked in a shaky voice, "What is it with you, anyway?"

When she opened her eyes, she saw that the sun shone in at an angle that reflected the struggle she was having and illuminated Jared, too. He stood on the spot where she had stomped away from him. He was perfectly still, then his shoulders drooped as if the burden he was carrying was breaking him down. His hand came up to his face.

Brittnie was so surprised at the change in him, she turned around. His eyes were squinted shut and he was pinching the bridge of his nose. "It's fear," he said in a dull voice.

Brittnie's eyes widened at this admission.

Jared dropped his hands to his sides and faced her. He shrugged as if he was momentarily helpless. The gesture, and the words coming from such a strong man, caught at her heart.

"It's fear," he repeated.

"Of…of what, exactly?" She took a few steps toward him. He moved to a sofa and perched on the edge of the seat, his elbows on his knees and his hands clasped loosely between them.

"He and I have always been close, more so than most grandfathers and grandsons. I suppose it's because I'm the only son of his only son. Until I became a teenager and decided it wasn't cool to be best friends with your grandfather, he and I were together every day."

Brittnie nodded, touched by the picture he painted of his relationship with Roberto.

"When I finished college, I realized he and I have the same interests: Business, real estate, property values, investments. We both like being in charge." He smiled in a self-deprecating way as if acknowledging she'd said that about him after the party at Roberto's house. "We seem to revel in taking on responsibility for people's property. Sometimes for their lives. Anyway, I joined the firm and we worked well together."

Brittnie, recalling the first encounter she had ever seen between them, put her hand on his arm. "Things were fine until he retired and you took charge."

"Yeah. We've been at odds for a year. He wants to keep his hand in, so he's been at the office every week, wanting to see the accounts, giving me advice on things he taught me years ago. It seems he can't let go and he can't quit. When he wasn't interfering in business matters, it was personal matters. He thinks I should move out of my condo and buy a house, get married, trade in my car. You name it and I've heard his opinion about it."

"He's afraid of being put out to pasture," Brittnie offered.

"I know, but ironically, he also wants to have time for himself. He needed something to occupy him which is why I came up with the idea of hiring someone qualified to sort Uncle David's things and take care of them. I knew it would keep him busy, but he still had to be careful of his heart."

Brittnie sighed. "I wish you'd told me all this three weeks ago. Why didn't you?"

He had the grace to look ashamed. "You were just an employee. I thought it was enough to tell you to watch out for him."

"Oh, Jared you are impossible," she moaned. She was silent for a minute, then she narrowed her eyes at him. "Since you're telling me this, what am I now?"

Jared reached over and took her hand. His was warm and vital, wrapping protectively around hers. "A friend who saved his life. Thank you."

Brittnie was touched again by his humble admission. "You're welcome," she whispered.

"And I'm saying all this now to explain that I've been acting like a frantic jerk because I'm afraid of losing him before he and I resolve things. I don't want to have regrets if he should...."

His voice trailed off and Brittnie's heart went out to him. She squeezed his hand. "I know what you mean. I've been sitting here having flashbacks of when my dad died. For weeks afterward, I went over every childish misdemeanor I'd ever committed against him, though I knew they were things he had long forgotten." Her throat closed unexpectedly against a tide of tears welling up. Embarrassed, she gave a small laugh and turned her face away. "I'm sorry," she choked. "I'm afraid I still do this sometimes when I think about him."

Jared put his arm around her and drew her close, then scooted them both back on the small sofa until she was held fast to his side and the top of her head was tucked beneath his chin. One last speck of sanity seemed to assert itself and Brittnie tried to struggle away, but he wouldn't let her go. Both of his arms came around to hold her firmly against him.

"Be still, Brittnie," he insisted. "Relax. We're going to sit here until the doctor comes. After he tells us the prognosis, I'll take you home."

Finally, she did as he said, surprised but grateful that he was being so understanding. As instructed, she let herself relax against him, savoring the feel of his arms around her and the scent of his spicy cologne. She knew that if she let herself think about the rightness or wrongness of this she would be struggling away from him, so she didn't think at all, allowing herself the incredible luxury of resting in his arms.

She could feel the steady beat of his heart against her ear. His breathing lifted her, then settled her back again. She knew when he swallowed.

She also knew the instant when all the emotions she had felt since first meeting Jared came together into one and she could give it a name. It was love. When it flashed across her mind, she stiffened.

"Hey," his voice rumbled against her ear. "Relax."

A shiver ran through her.

"Are you cold?"

"No," she whispered, then cleared her throat. "No. I'm f-fine." What a lie that was, she thought hysterically as he settled back. Eyes wide, she stared at the wall opposite them. She had never been less fine. She had never been more distraught.

When did this happen? How could it have happened? Brittnie's mind raced, trying to pinpoint the instant she'd fallen in love with him. The day they'd met in that elevator, when he had put Steve Wilberson in his place? Maybe it had been the night they'd scared the daylights out of each other in David's house, then gone out for a late supper. Could it have been when he kissed her?

Her reactions to him suddenly came into focus. If she'd been in love with him all along, it explained why she became so incensed with him when he didn't seem to trust her and had thrust so much unreasonable responsibility on her for the care of his grandfather. Unconsciously, she'd wanted him to feel the same way about her and if he'd trusted her, that meant he loved her.

Loving Jared Cruz? What a stupid thing to do.

She had to begin dealing with this, and the sooner the better. Shakily, she sat up, pushing herself away from him, scooting across the slick vinyl seat. "I'm all right now," she said, not daring to meet his eyes for fear he would read something there that she didn't want him to see.

She was rescued from further agonizing when Roberto's doctor strolled into the waiting room. Instantly, she and Jared were both on their feet.

"There doesn't seem to be any further damage to his heart," the doctor reported. "And if he takes care of himself, he'll live a long time yet."

Relieved, Jared and Brittnie slumped against each other. "That's good," Jared said. His arm came around Brittnie's shoulders, and hers went around his waist for mutual support.

"He's resting and he must keep resting," the doctor added bluntly. "He's got to be here in the hospital for a few days, then another week resting at home." He went on to explain what to expect in Roberto's recovery, told them they could visit him, then strode out at a fast clip.

Brittnie hung back, but Jared grabbed her hand and pulled her with him. "Granddad will expect to see you," he said. Nodding, she followed along. Jared didn't waste any time finding Roberto's room. A nurse was just leaving, and told them not to be long.

They stood on each side of Roberto's bed, looked down at his pale face, then at each other. She knew that if her expression was as ghastly as Jared's, they would frighten poor Roberto into another attack. "Smile," she mouthed at him, just as Roberto's eyes fluttered open.

His gaze landed on Brittnie's face. "Sorry I scared you, honey."

"I'm sorry you got sick," she answered, reaching for his hand which lay on top of the bedcovers. It was cool to her touch, but felt far more natural than the frightening clamminess she'd noticed before.

Roberto's eyes swung to Jared, who managed to smooth his features and force a slight smile before meeting his grandfather's gaze.

"Don't say it," Roberto warned, his dark eyes challenging Jared.

"I don't think I need to," Jared answered, his expression rueful. The light was dim in the room, with only a faint glow coming from a lamp near Roberto's head. In its pale illumination, Brittnie could see how Jared's face softened.

Roberto sighed. "No. I know I've been a fool, but I wanted to see what was in that last journal, you know what I mean?" His tone was breathy with longing.

"Yes, of course, but it's not worth risking your health."

"I didn't think I was," Roberto said. "It's hard to admit when you're getting old and...." He looked at Jared, then at Brittnie. "And running out of time," he concluded.

A protest formed on Brittnie's lips, but a look from him kept her from voicing it. There was no point in saying something they both knew wasn't true. She swallowed, but there was a lump in her throat.

"You'll have lots of time left, Granddad," Jared told him. Brittnie knew he was trying to be firm and hearty, but it sounded forced. "If you'll stop this foolishness."

Roberto released a long sigh. "You're right. I never should have started the search for that last journal. I'll give it up, follow the doctor's orders, and behave myself.

I'll even go stay with John and Miranda in Phoenix this winter like all of you have been wanting me to.''

Jared straightened and looked down at his grandfather as if he'd been handed a wonderful gift. His eyes shot up to Brittnie, who answered with a relieved smile of her own. "Granddad, that's...that's great.''

"If you'll finish the search for me.''

"What?''

"You've never been hard of hearing, boy. You finish the search for me. Find me that journal so I'll know....'' His voice trailed off and he closed his eyes briefly, then opened them again, focusing on Jared. "Find it for me.''

Jared's face fell. "I can't do that. I've got a business to run.''

Roberto snorted, though it sounded weak. "We both know Sandra could run the company with one hand tied behind her back.''

"That may be overstating it just a little. Besides, you've had problems letting *me* run it this past year.''

Roberto didn't respond to that. Instead, he said, "Finding the journal won't take that long. A couple of weeks.''

"Granddad, I don't think so....''

Roberto ignored that. "You'll need to stay at the house, too, like Brittnie does. That way you can spend more time looking, you won't be distracted by business, and you won't have interruptions.''

This time both Jared and Brittnie gaped at him. Her first surge of emotion was stark terror. They couldn't spend that much time together. What if Jared found out how she felt about him? It was followed by intense joy at the thought of being alone with him, for even a few days.

Jared looked at her and she saw something flicker in

his eyes. It was quickly shuttered, but it seemed to reflect what was in her mind.

Jared cleared his throat. "Granddad, I don't think that's a good idea."

"Oh, forget what I said the other night about you needing to marry this girl," the older man insisted. "It was foolish talk."

"I wasn't thinking of that."

Roberto lifted his hand. Brittnie knew he was trying for one of his usual, careless waves, but he didn't have the strength to manage it.

"Roberto, we're tiring you out. I know you're anxious about that journal, but why don't we talk more when you feel better?" She hustled around the bed, grabbed Jared's arm, and started for the door. He mumbled a goodbye to his grandfather, and came along, though not willingly. Brittnie whipped the door open, shoved him outside, then hiked down the hall with him in tow.

"I can't believe he asked me to do that," Jared said, reaching up to release the death grip she had on his sleeve. "I can't just take time off to rummage around in that musty old house."

"And why should you when you can hire someone to do it for you?" Brittnie asked. "Someone like me."

If Jared heard her sardonic tone, he chose to ignore it. His jaw took on the stubborn set she was coming to recognize as a Cruz family characteristic. "I don't have time."

"Neither does he."

Jared winced as if his conscience had just kicked him.

By now they had reached the elevator. Brittnie punched the button for the ground floor and stepped inside. They were alone, so they returned to the argument. "This is obviously important to him."

"I know that."

"I don't think you do. You wanted him to be involved in sorting his brother's things so he would be out of your hair."

"I never made a secret of that, but mainly I wanted to please him."

She stared at him. "And now you no longer want to please him because it will take some of your time?" she asked incredulously. "Are you the same man who just told me you want to repair your relationship with him?"

Jared gave her a hard look, then he stepped to the back of the elevator, crossed his arms, and drummed his fingertips against his biceps. After a moment, his lips twitched, his face softened, and he said, "I hate it when you're right."

Brittnie grinned and lifted her hands in a shrug. "And it happens so often, too. I know it must be hard for you to take."

"Smart mouth."

"Look on the bright side. The journal might turn up tomorrow. It might be on top of the next box or chest we open."

"Does the saying 'fat chance' have any meaning for you?"

Brittnie laughed as they stepped from the elevator. They started for the parking lot where Jared had left his car.

"You'll let him know you plan to finish the search?"

"Yes."

"And, um, the other part of it?"

"You mean moving into the house?"

"Yes." Brittnie kept her eyes averted as he unlocked the car door for her and helped her inside.

"Is there a bedroom available?"

Yes, mine. Appalled by what she had almost blurted, Brittnie took a breath and said, "Yes, but the ones upstairs would have to be cleared out. There's one downstairs, behind the kitchen. It has its own bathroom. I think it must have been a servant's room at some time in the past. The cleaning crew you sent cleaned both rooms."

He nodded, but he didn't say anything more.

As they drove back to David's house, Brittnie's mind ran in frantic circles, wondering if he would, indeed, move into the house with her. Part of her realized it made simple common sense for him to do so, but another part was aghast at the idea. How could she keep her feelings hidden, treat him in a professional manner, or even a breezy, friendly one without wearing her heart on her sleeve? She had never been good at hiding her emotions. How could she hide this one, the biggest one of all? Already it was trying to burst from her.

She looked out the window as street signs, homes, and businesses passed. The only thing to do was to abandon the book cataloging she'd been working on and help him find the journal. That way, he would be out of the house and out of her life that much sooner.

And she wasn't going to even think about how much that idea hurt.

When the doorbell rang at seven o'clock that evening, Brittnie rushed down, to let Jared in. She had showered and changed into clean slacks and a matching top in sunny yellow and twisted her hair into a loose knot on top of her head. She had spent ten minutes trying to convince herself that she wasn't dressing up because he was coming, then gave it up and began putting on makeup and looking for her jade earrings. She did manage to stop herself from spritzing on the Chanel No.5 Becca had given her for her birthday.

Jared carried a duffel bag and a sleeping bag. He no longer wore the charcoal suit he'd had on at the hospital. In fact, he was dressed more casually than she'd ever seen him in jeans and a dark blue T-shirt.

When he swept in the front door and said, "I talked to Granddad. He's relieved I'm carrying on with this for him."

"I knew he would be," Brittnie said faintly, aware that seeing him was having its usual affect on her. At least now she knew what was causing it.

"I'll stow this stuff in the bedroom, then we can get to work."

She barely heard him. Her hand released the doorknob and it started to swing shut as she slowly turned and watched him disappear through the dining room.

Her mouth had gone dry and her eyes couldn't seem to tear themselves away from the sight of him in that T-shirt. He did all the right things to a shirt like that, she thought, stretching it in exactly the places where it was supposed to be stretched.

The rearview of him in those jeans wasn't bad, either. In fact, it was just about guaranteed to raise her temperature a few notches.

Fanning her throat with her hand, she decided that she'd been a snob about men with desk jobs. Obviously, he did something to keep himself in great shape. She already knew he worked too hard, spent too much time in his office. His grandfather called him a workaholic, but Jared worked at something else, too. Muscles like those didn't appear by accident.

Before she had time to recover, he had loped back into the entryway where she still stood by the door.

Looking around expectantly, he said, "Where do we start?"

She blinked at him. "Excuse me?"

"It won't work if we duplicate each other's efforts, so tell me where you've already searched and I'll start somewhere else."

"You mean tonight?"

He had been prowling the entryway, poking his nose in the library door, then the living room. Now he turned to face her with a puzzled look on his face. "Sure. Why not? It's barely past seven."

Brittnie opened her mouth to protest, then snapped it shut, swallowing her dismay. What could she say? After all, he wasn't here to see her. He was here to work. She had to stop being so absolutely foolish, to quit day-dreaming like a lovesick teenager. She *knew* there was no way that there could ever be anything between them except a professional relationship, maybe even friend-ship. So, why was it she couldn't convince her heart?

She pressed her palms together at her waist, trying to stabilize the lump of disappointment that had plunged down from her throat. "Of course we can start now. No reason not to. No reason at all."

He frowned at her. "Something wrong, Brittnie? You've got a strange look on your face. You feeling okay?" He stepped closer. "Hey, I'm a dunce. I didn't even think that you might be having a reaction to all of the excitement today."

She was having a reaction, all right, but not the one he thought. Jared clasped her arm and hustled her over to the sofa. He sat her down, then sat beside her, edged his knee onto the sofa cushion and half turned toward her. "Forget what I said. We can start tomorrow morn-ing." He turned in place, searching the room. "You need to do something to relax. How about watching television?''

Brittnie smiled. "Good luck. Your great-uncle didn't have one."

Jared's head snapped around. "A house full of every imaginable object on earth, but no television?"

"From what I've seen, it was probably a little too modern for his taste." She pointed to an overflowing cabinet in the corner. "There's a radio, and there are some games in there."

"Games?" He gave her a skeptical look. "You mean like board games?"

"That's right."

"I don't play games."

"Too busy working?" Her tone was a breath away from being a taunt.

He shrugged. "Yeah, usually."

She pursed her lips, placed her palms on her knees and locked her elbows in a stretch. Her gray eyes laughed at him from beneath her lashes. "You know what they say about all work and no play."

Jared leaned closer. "You saying I'm dull?"

"Oh, I wouldn't go that far."

"Just dim, maybe?"

She grinned, but she didn't answer.

"You do a lot for a man's ego," he groused. Standing, he moved to the cabinet where he began sifting through the games. "Ah, here we go." He turned back to her with a Monopoly set in his hands.

"You would choose the one that involves your area of expertise," she said.

"I don't see one here that has to do with obscure literary facts. Besides, you don't have to own a property management firm to play this game."

"Though it would help," she murmured as he removed the game board from its worn box and began parceling out the play money. While he was busy with that, she went into the kitchen and sliced pieces of her mother's German chocolate cake for them. His eyes lit up when he saw it and the two of them settled down for a friendly game of Monopoly.

Within half an hour, he owned seven hotels. She had one and almost no money.

Brittnie crossed her arms at her waist and gave him a hard look. "Are you cheating?"

His expression was full of innocence, but his brown eyes had a devilish sparkle. "Oh, come on. How could I cheat? You're sitting right across from me. You're watching every move I make like an eagle waiting for a mouse."

"Humph. I don't think I'm watching you closely enough. Are those trick dice?"

He tossed them into the air and then reached out to grab her hand and drop them into her palm. "You're using the same dice."

"Yeah, well, they're not being very lucky for me."

"I don't think you're concentrating. Great financial minds have an unusual ability to concentrate," he said in a pompous tone.

"And they also have the ability to annoy the heck out of people." She rolled the dice and went back to playing.

Half an hour later, she'd bought out most of his hotels and was rolling in cash.

"Are you letting me win?" she asked suspiciously.

He threw his hands in the air. "I give up. Either I'm cheating, or I'm letting you win. Believe it or not, this is actually a game of chance and strategy."

She sat back and considered him for a minute.

"You're right. And by chance, I've won. Let's quit. It's getting late."

Jared sputtered with indignation. "When *you're* winning, it's time to quit?"

"It's one of the rules," she said innocently. "It's printed right there on the inside of the box lid."

He picked it up and peered at it, squinting to read the small print. "You lie," he said, tossing it aside.

"That's insulting." She grabbed it and, leaning close to him, pointed to something printed at the bottom. "Right there."

"That's the trademark."

Feigning surprise, she held it close to her face. "Well, I'll be darned. I think you're right."

Laughing, Jared made a grab for the lid, but she held it away, teasing him. He swooped in, clasping her around the waist and jerking her toward him as he snagged the lid from her hand. He tossed it toward the box, then spun her around to face him.

In the tussle, Brittnie's hair came loose, tendrils falling down around her face. Jared trapped both her wrists in one of his hands and, with the other, reached up to push her hair back. His eyes were speculative, warmed by some inner heat that seemed to perplex him. "You're quite a woman, Brittnie Kelleher. You make me forget...."

"Forget what?" she asked in a breathless tone.

He shook his head as if the words wouldn't form for what he wanted to say. "Work," he finally said. "Responsibilities."

"That's what games, board games, are for."

"It wasn't the game. It was you." His voice and his gaze were steady, but his hands trembled around hers.

Brittnie felt herself swaying toward him. Oh, Lord,

she wanted his arms around her, his mouth on hers. She wanted him to return the love she felt and for them both to forget the barriers between them. Her conscience pricked at her. She couldn't do that, though, because the barriers would still be there.

With an effort, she pulled her hands from his and stepped back. "Well, that's...that's enough games for tonight. We'd better go to...I mean *I'd* better go to bed. Lots of work to do tomorrow."

"Brittnie, it's nine o'clock. I find it hard to believe that you go to bed this early. Aren't you afraid you'll wake up at two in the morning with insomnia?"

She swallowed. "Uh, no. This is something new I've started."

"I'll bet."

She turned and fled toward the staircase, knowing he was watching every move. His, "Good night, Brittnie," drifted up the stairs, but she didn't respond. She was too busy running away from him and from the thought of the coming days, or weeks, when this would be their nightly ritual.

And she wanted so much more.

CHAPTER EIGHT

"WHAT, exactly, are we looking for?"

Brittnie glanced up from the books she had spent the week cataloging. She was trying to get them cleared away so that she could help Jared with his search. She had known people in her field who would leave stacks of books and papers—sometimes very important papers lying around, but she couldn't do that. Everything needed to be carefully placed so that she would know where to find it when she returned to it.

Unfortunately, Jared hadn't wanted to wait until she was finished and had started without her. He had been nosing around the library while she worked, scanning the bookshelves and poking into the file cabinets, then slamming the drawers shut so that she jumped with each bang. He had examined the shelves of curios and picked up each candlestick, figurine, and paperweight that lined the mantel.

He was driving her crazy.

She didn't even want to think about how crazy he'd driven her last night, though he hadn't done a thing. Just knowing he was sleeping downstairs, and she upstairs had been enough to disturb her.

And this morning, carrying on with her recently discovered tendency toward total idiocy, she had dressed in her favorite blue tank top and shorts because the color put azure highlights in her eyes. She knew he hadn't dressed to please her, but she was pleased, anyway. His T-shirt was red, a color she never would have associated with him, and it was tucked into the same snug jeans he had worn the night before. She was coming to love those jeans.

Reaching across the desk, she picked up one of the dark green journals. "One like this," she said.

He took it from her, flipped it open, took one look at the writing and crossed his eyes comically. He handed it back. "They're all like that?"

Brittnie laughed at his expression. "All the others have been these green-bound books, but that's no guarantee that the last one will be," she admitted. "I'm hoping it is, but he might have used a different type of journal or notebook, even sheets of paper if such things as notebooks and journals were growing hard to find. I don't know where he was at the end of the war so I don't know what kinds of supplies he had access to."

Jared grinned. "Researched it, did you?"

"That's my job," she answered with a smirk and a flutter of her eyelashes that made *him* laugh this time.

She went back to what she had been doing and he took another turn around the room.

"I think you're going about this all wrong," he said suddenly.

"Excuse me?"

"I said you're going about this all wrong," he responded, standing in the middle of the room, hands resting on his waist as he surveyed the area like an explorer ready to stake his claim for king and country.

Brittnie gave him a wary look. She didn't like the acquisitive light in his eyes. "What specifically?"

"Now that I look at this, I think the way you're going about it could stand some improvement."

"Do you mean the journal search specifically, or the entire job you hired me for?"

"Just this room. The library." He gestured to the books that lined the walls and were stacked on every surface including the floor.

"Oh, really? What did you have in mind?" She couldn't imagine why she'd asked that. She truly didn't want to know.

"A more efficient system. Something that will get more work done in a shorter amount of time."

If he would leave the room, she could get more work done in a shorter amount of time, but she only gave him a politely curious look—which was a mistake because it only encouraged him.

He crossed his arms over his chest and turned slowly. "Wouldn't it go faster if you put them all in alphabetical order by author, then cataloged them?"

Brittnie shuddered at the thought. "Only if I wanted to drive myself insane. Jared, most of these books only need to be sorted, then leafed through once to see if they contain anything important. Your great-uncle had a habit of picking up anything handy and using it for a book-mark. Yesterday, I found a World War II gas rationing card in a volume of *Oliver Twist*. After they're sorted, the books will be donated to schools and libraries. Roberto wants to keep the rarest ones and the ones that belonged to his parents. I'll catalog those. That's what I'm doing now. He thinks you might want them some-day." She emphasized the last sentence, but Jared only nodded. He had his mind on other things.

"I see. So you've already culled out the ones he wants?"

"Mostly, yes."

Jared turned to the first floor-to-ceiling bookcase in the room. "Then we should be able to tear through these in record time." He began pulling books from the shelf, giving them a cursory look, then stacking them on the floor.

The words "tear through" had Brittnie leaping from her chair. She vaulted across the room, her hands stretched out to stop the impending chaos. "Wait, Jared. We've got to be careful."

"I'm being careful." Another stack of books thumped down.

Brittnie winced, pained by his carelessness. "We have a duty to treat these books well...."

"They're paper, ink, and glue," he said, skimming several more volumes before adding them to his growing stack. "Not babies."

"They might as well be."

Her mournful tone finally caught his attention and he looked up, startled. "You really mean that."

"They're valuable," she said accusingly.

"Like first editions, you mean?"

She rolled her eyes heavenward and prayed for strength. "No. They're valuable because of what they contain. Books hold all the knowledge of mankind. They deserve to be maintained. They're valuable," she said again.

"Brittnie, I love to read," he said defensively.

She leveled a stare at him.

"Really," he said, raising his hands to proclaim his honesty. "I like books, but I don't get sentimental over them."

"A blind man could see that," she huffed.

Distressed, she stooped to pick up the ones that had landed on the floor. He paused for a second. She could feel his eyes on her for long seconds before he crouched down beside her, and took the volumes from her hands. Her lips pinched in a pained look, she tried to take them back. Jared held on to them and covered her hands with his own. She looked up.

His brown eyes darkened as they searched her face. "This is pretty important to you."

"It needs to be done right. That's what you're paying me for."

The corner of his mouth kicked up in a smile. "And you know the right way."

"I didn't spend six years going to school, waiting tables to put myself through, so that I could make a mess on my first job."

"No, of course not. I understand."

No, he didn't. He'd probably had his education handed to him, and while she didn't begrudge that, she wasn't sure he understood what she was trying to say. She took a breath and tried again.

"Some people become librarians because they're interested in all types of media, or because they like doing research, or, believe it or not, some people think it will be an easy, cushy job where they spend their days pointing patrons to books they'll enjoy or helping them get access to the Internet." She took a breath and barreled ahead. "Most librarians choose the profession because they like books and everything to do with books. I'm one of those. I like handing a child a book and watching their eyes when they come back to tell me how much they loved it. Also, I've got a great-aunt, Katrina, who was a librarian. It's in my blood."

"Brittnie...." He tried to interrupt, but she had a full head of steam up.

"I like books," she said, passion trembling in her voice. "Thick, thin, enormous, I like them. Tiny volumes of poetry and big, fat dictionaries. It doesn't matter. I like the way they feel and smell. I like the things they tell me, the things I can learn. The world would be lost without books.'' She shrugged. ''I feel like I have a duty to preserve them if I can.''

His hands tightened on hers. ''Brittnie, I can see that.''

She looked away, embarrassed that she'd let herself get so carried away. She hadn't meant to.

''I'm sorry,'' he went on. ''I'm that take-charge, bull-by-the-horns guy, remember?''

''Yeah, I've noticed. Only today you're more like a bull in a china shop.''

He winced, but he didn't deny it. ''I noticed something about you,'' he said, quiet teasing in his voice. ''When you're nervous or upset, words pour out of you like water from the spring snow melt.''

Not a flattering description, she decided, but an accurate one. ''Yes, they do.''

He tugged on her hands, drawing her closer into the vee formed by his knees. He leaned in as if to give her a kiss on the cheek. Startled, Brittnie's head came up and the kiss landed on her lips.

It was light, the merest touch, but the spark and sizzle were instantaneous as if electricity had shot through them both.

Eyes wide, looking straight into his, her mouth a half breath away, she whispered, ''What was that?''

He didn't blink. ''Trouble.''

She breathed in, bringing his essence inside. ''We got this out of our systems,'' she said, shakily. ''Days ago. Remember?''

''I remember.''

''We proved there was no attraction so that Roberto wouldn't get any ideas.''

"He's already got ideas," Jared pointed out, closing the gap between them. "And he's not here."

His lips were feather light against hers, his touch tentative as if she was a shy creature he didn't want to frighten away. While his lips held her captive, his hands encouraged hers to leave the stack of books she held. She released the volumes to him and heard them slip quietly to the floor. Then his hands were on her shoulders, drawing her up until they stood face to face, mouth to mouth. His fingers kneaded her muscles, reaching beneath the narrow shoulder straps of her tank top. Then his arms were around her, drawing her in as he deepened the kiss.

Brittnie went willingly, molding herself to him as his lips devoured hers. She loved this, loved him, loved the way his hands seemed to cherish her. She'd never felt this way before, perhaps because she'd never felt this way about a man before. No one had made her feel treasured like this, excited and drunk with joy like this.

Delight ran through her in rivers, flooding out from her. Her hands were at his waist, but they moved up, clutching handfuls of his T-shirt, then spreading her palms wide to knead the muscles that banded his back.

"Ah, Brittnie." His voice was raw and harsh.

She wanted to tell him all the feelings that were rushing through her, but all she could say was his name, "Jared."

"This is nice," he murmured. "More than nice."

She chuckled at the understatement. It was wonderful.

"I like kissing a woman my height. Saves me from neck strain."

Her laugh got caught in her throat when he placed a kiss there. Hazily, she thought that the other women he kissed must be short. She froze. Of course they were. At least one was. Linda. Shame and panic chased away the desire she'd been feeling.

"Ja…Jared." She stopped and gulped for breath as she pulled her tingling lips away from his. "Jared, stop."

His eyes were closed. His mouth returning to hers. "In a minute."

She held him away. "Now."

"Why?" His breathing was as ragged as hers.

"Linda," she said desperately. "Your fiancée, Linda."

An emotion flared in his eyes. Irritation, she thought, and it was directed at her. "She…."

"She doesn't deserve to be treated like this," Brittnie said quickly. She drew her trembling fingers across her lips. "And neither do I."

Anger replaced irritation in his face. "You weren't complaining a minute ago."

She forced herself to meet his eyes. "No. I…like being kissed by you." She put her chin up. "I'd like a lot more from you, but this is going to stop. Now. It's wrong."

He looked as if he wanted to argue with her. Brittnie knew he couldn't because she was right. If he hadn't been a man of honor, he would have argued with her. He seemed to fight a battle with himself and honor won. "You're right," he said, stepping back. He ran a hand through his hair and turned away. "Hell, I'm not going to be like your buddy Steve Wilberson." He stooped to pick up the books he'd dropped on the floor.

Brittnie folded as if she'd been punched in the stomach. Hurt, and appalled at him, she started to protest, but she stopped herself. Did he mean he wouldn't try to cheat on Linda the way Steve had tried to cheat on

Lauren? Or was it something else? Surely he didn't think she had led Steve on? Had led *him* on? Angry denial sprang to her lips, but she bit it back. Anything she said would only prolong the argument and they both needed to back away from this situation, from this awareness that was growing between them and ruining everything.

Brittnie loved him. She could accept that. He didn't love her, but he desired her. She could also accept that as long as it went no further.

Pulling air into her lungs, she straightened inch by inch until she was at her full height. Ignoring everything that had happened between them in the past few minutes, she said, "I don't know what you meant by that."

His head snapped around.

She lifted a hand to stall him. "And I don't want to know. Let's just forget it."

"Sure," he said, sarcasm lining his tone. "Piece of cake." Savagely, he leaned forward and gripped the front edge of a shelf on the bookcase. "I'm sorry, Brittnie. This is a hell of a mess."

Her anger with him began to evaporate into confusion. She didn't know what he was thinking, what emotions were driving him. She certainly didn't know what his feelings were toward her—except desire. That was undeniable. And it wasn't enough.

She lifted her chin. "I suggest we come up with a plan for the search. If you start here, I'll begin with the bookcases in the living room. Some of them haven't been touched in years. It could be there."

Jared placed the last of the books on the shelf and slapped them into place with his palm. "Whatever you say, boss."

She hurried out and made a beeline for the living room. Quickly and methodically, she began searching through the accumulated items that were crammed onto the shelves. The faster she found the journal, the faster Jared would be going, and it couldn't be soon enough for her.

Jared and Brittnie took a break for a strained and quiet lunch, then went right back to work with him in the library and her in the living room. When Brittnie heard a knock at the door a short time later, she uncurled herself from her cramped position before a low hutch stuffed with books and papers. She had to stop and massage a spasm in her calf and by the time she reached the door, the caller had knocked two more times.

She opened the door to find Linda Pomfort on the porch. She was dressed in a spring green sundress with matching shoes and a picture hat as if she was returning from a garden party. Brittnie, hot, sweaty, and dusty could only stare at such polished perfection.

"Hello," Linda said, giving Brittnie a quick, thorough look, then dismissing her as she craned her neck to look into the house. "Brittnie, isn't it? Is Jared here?"

Brittnie stepped back and waved toward the library. "You'll find him in there." As soon as Linda moved inside, Brittnie shut the door and went back to work. Although she tried to ignore them, she heard the low murmur of voices. When she went to the kitchen for a glass of water a few minutes later, she heard Linda's voice low and insistent.

"You've got to let me do this, Jared," she was saying. "I...need your help."

"Linda, you need to help yourself...."

"Not yet." The girl's voice held a hint of panic.

Brittnie would have loved to hear more, but she forced herself to keep walking. It was none of her business, or so she thought until Jared appeared in the kitchen doorway a few minutes later, Linda right behind him.

With surprise, Brittnie noted the uncomfortable look on his face. "Is something wrong?"

"We have a...situation," he said.

Standing beside him, Linda nodded. She regarded Brittnie with a triumphant look. Brittnie returned her attention to Jared. "Oh?"

"Yes." He rocked up onto his toes, then back on his heels as he pushed his palms together in front of him.

Good grief, Brittnie realized in amazement. *He's nervous.*

"Linda wants to come and stay while I'm here."

You're kidding, Brittnie thought, but again, she said, "Oh?"

Linda reached up and tucked her hand into the crook of Jared's elbow. "If we're going to be married, I think I ought to be here. I mean, it doesn't look right for him to be living here with you when he's going to marry me."

Brittnie blinked, still unable to take this in. "Stay?" she asked. "Here?" Would she and Jared be sharing a room?

Jared gave Brittnie a look that told her he was reading her mind. It was direct, and challenging, but when he gazed at Linda, his expression softened. "I thought she could have that back bedroom upstairs," he said, flashing Brittnie another glance.

"It's full of boxes. The bed isn't made," Brittnie floundered.

"You can clear the room and make the bed, can't you?" Linda scoffed.

Brittnie stared. *"Me?"*

"We'll do it, Linda," Jared said. When she started to

protest, he gave her a firm look. "If you want to stay, you'll get your own room ready."

Her lips pinched in irritation, but she subsided.

Brittnie cast around for something polite to say, though Linda wasn't making much of an effort to be polite to her. She finally managed, "You're...you're welcome here. After all, this is Jared's house—in a way. We'll be glad of your help."

Linda tittered. Her stunning green eyes fluttered up to Jared, then back to Brittnie. "Oh, I won't be here to *work*."

Heaven forbid, Brittnie thought. *Can't let that happen.* She recovered herself, nodded slowly and said, "I see."

"I have things to do," Linda chirped. "In fact, you won't see me much at all."

Then why be here? Brittnie gave Jared a questioning look, but his attention was on his fiancée and he didn't see it.

"I have my things in the car," Linda said brightening. "Jared, can you help me bring them in?"

"Sure." He turned and strode out. Linda took one look at Brittnie's puzzled face and scurried after him.

Her need for a drink of water forgotten, Brittnie trailed along to see what would happen next. Jared propped the front door open and went out to Linda's car. Eyes wide, Brittnie watched him remove two large suitcases and three smaller ones from the car. Brittnie couldn't imagine how Linda had managed to wedge them inside— unless, of course, she had someone else do it for her.

Jared came up the steps with the two largest suitcases. Linda waited by the car, giving Brittnie an expectant look. Brittnie knew her expression told Linda that she'd better think again about expecting help from her. After a moment, Linda ducked her head, grabbed two small suitcases, and followed Jared. She strode past Brittnie with her nose in the air and trotted up the stairs. Dismayed, Brittnie returned to the living room, sat down on the floor and considered bursting into tears.

This was unbelievable. Who but Brittnie Kelleher could do something as dumb as fall in love with an engaged man? Who but she would have the bad luck to stay in the same house with the engaged couple?

Within moments, she heard the sounds of boxes being dragged from the bedroom, then thumping and bumping as the furniture was rearranged. Brittnie had a pretty good idea who was doing all that work. Linda was probably standing by, directing.

Brittnie reminded herself yet again that it was none of her business. She should resign, she thought, automatically pulling several books from the crammed shelves and scanning them for the journal she sought. She should resign from this whole strange operation. The heck with David Cruz's crazy, crowded house. She nodded, liking the sound of that phrase. The heck with digging through all this stuff for a journal that had probably been thrown away years ago. The heck with making a name for herself, with building her career. The heck with her career.

"She won't be any trouble," Jared said from the doorway.

Brittnie jumped and whipped her head around. She'd been so involved in feeling sorry for herself, she hadn't heard him come in. She took a breath and blew her bangs out of her face. "Is that a promise?"

He came into the room and stood towering over her. Unwilling to allow that, Brittnie scrambled to her feet to face him.

"Jared, your personal life is your business," she said,

then winced at the triteness of that phrase. "But this is a workplace." Her hands flew out to encompass the room. "I have work to do, and I thought that was what you're here for."

His chin came out in its stubborn way. "I'm here because I fulfill my responsibilities—and my promises." Turning, he strode out, returning to the library and closing the door.

Whatever that meant, Brittnie thought. Her mind in turmoil and her heart aching, she followed his example and got back to work. She didn't see either of her fellow housemates for the remainder of the afternoon, which suited her just fine. She'd had enough shocks for one day and wanted to concentrate on work. If she could.

Jared and Linda went out that evening. Brittnie told herself she didn't know or care where they'd gone. She had been in the kitchen, rummaging through the refrigerator for her own dinner, but she'd peeked out the front window when the sound of the closing front door drew her to the entryway and the long, narrow windows on each side of the door.

They hadn't told her they were leaving, but then, they didn't have to. She peeked out and had been interested to see that Jared had been dressed in slacks, white shirt, and a sport coat and Linda had been wearing one of her lovely dresses. This one was teal green. Didn't the girl own a pair of jeans? Brittnie wondered, looking down at her own dusty shorts outfit. She groaned.

She had to get out of this house and do something fun or she would sit around and indulge in another pity party. Hurrying back to the kitchen, she ate a cold dinner, then went upstairs for a shower and change of clothes. She defiantly got dressed up in clean white slacks that fit snugly enough to show off her long, shapely legs, and a sunny yellow silk shirt that tied at her waist. She would go see Shannon, she decided as she applied her makeup, or she would call Timmy and Ben and see if they wanted to go out, or failing those options, she could drive out to Tarrant and see her sister Becca. She hadn't played video games with her nephew, Jimmy, in weeks. She was due for a visit. Besides, she should check on Becca, see how her sister was feeling, how her pregnancy was coming along.

She had plenty to do, Brittnie thought. Plenty. She didn't have to sit around while life passed her by and the man she was silly enough to love was out with someone else. She was busy. She had friends who would be glad of a call from her. She could go anywhere, do anything.

She ended up at the hospital visiting Roberto.

He was thrilled to see her, dropping the magazine he'd been reading onto a big stack on a side table and motioning her inside.

"Come in, Brittnie. Come in. John and Miranda have been here all day. They just left to go to my house so I'm all alone."

Brittnie glanced at the clock as she sat down. "I can't stay long. Visiting hours are almost over and I don't want to tire you out."

"You won't." He smoothed the light sheet over his legs. "Now, tell me. Did you find the missing journal?"

"No, I'm sorry, we haven't yet, but we're still looking. It may take quite some time," she warned.

"I know. That's what Jared said."

"Oh, he's been here?" Brittnie turned aside and pretended interest in a basket of flowers that had been placed on the table by her chair. She could see the card. They were from Jared and Linda.

"Yes," the older man growled. "With Linda. I know she depends on him, but she runs to him with every little problem. It's ridiculous."

Brittnie didn't answer, though she was tempted to agree. "Well, maybe after she's been at David's house for a while, she'll see that and want to be self-sufficient."

"At David's house?" Roberto sat up straight. "You mean she's moved in? With you and Jared?"

"Why, yes," Brittnie said, then her voice trailed off into a tiny squeak. "They didn't tell you, did they?"

"Not a word. She doesn't need to be there. She needs to leave. The girl has got to stand on her own two feet sometime."

Alarmed, Brittnie jumped up to hover over the bed. "Roberto, please don't excite yourself."

"Too late. I'm already excited." He crossed his arms over his chest. "Well, obviously I need to do something about this," he said, huffily. "There's only one solution."

Full of dread, Brittnie asked, "And what would that be?"

"I'll hire a nurse to watch out for me, help me, and I'll move in, too, for as long as Linda is there."

CHAPTER NINE

"WHY did you tell him?"

"I didn't tell him intentionally. I thought he knew since you and Linda had already been there to see him."

Brittnie and Jared had been having this discussion for fifteen minutes already and she didn't see any end in sight. For crying out loud, the man was like a bulldog with a beef bone in his teeth. "It just slipped out," she went on. "I certainly didn't do it deliberately."

They were in the living room. Brittnie was perched on the edge of the sofa cushion and Jared was pacing the room—not an easy task because he had to continually dodge the furniture, but he still managed to whip back and forth like a caged panther hoping to have filet of zookeeper for lunch.

She had come straight home after her visit with Roberto because she knew she would have to face Jared and she didn't want to take a chance that he might hear it from Roberto himself. Even though she hadn't revealed the news on purpose, she was still responsible.

Jared and Linda had arrived a few minutes later. Brittnie had been surprised to see that it looked as if the two of them were at odds. Jared's jaw was set and Linda's face was red and agitated. When she saw that Brittnie was waiting to speak to Jared, she hesitated as if she was reluctant to leave the two of them alone. Her irritation with him must have overcome her hesitation because after a moment, she went upstairs.

Brittnie had immediately dropped her bombshell on

148

Jared. They had been arguing in hushed tones ever since—and she hadn't even told him the worst part yet. She'd better get that over with, as well.

"Jared, I'm sorry. I admit this is my fault, but I'm not finished," she finally said, holding up her hand to halt his pacing. "You haven't heard all of it."

His eyes widened. "There's *more?*"

She clasped her hands together. She had never been one to sit and wring her hands, but this looked like a good time to start. Her eye full of regret, she said, "He's going to move in, too. With a nurse." She couldn't help squeezing her eyes shut and hunching her shoulders as if waiting for an explosion. When it didn't come, she opened her eyes again.

Jared stared at her for a full minute as the impact of her words hit him. Then he clasped the top of his head between his palms and said, "Ooo-ooh *man!*" He stalked across the room to stand in front of her.

Brittnie jumped to her feet. She tried to form a placating smile, but it slipped away. "Now, Jared, there's no reason to get upset...."

"No reason?" he interrupted. His face was growing red and Brittnie was fascinated to see that the angrier he got, the more a vein on the side of his neck popped out. She would have to look for that sign in the future. "There's every reason. He's supposed to be home resting, not here sticking his nose in our business."

"He thinks it *is* his business." She began rubbing her temples where a tension headache was beginning to thud. "He seems to think everything is his business."

"Now you're catching on." Jared scraped a hand across his hair and took another turn around the room.

Brittnie watched him for a few minutes, giving him time to cool down before she went on. "Jared, I talked for twenty minutes trying to convince him not to do this, but he wouldn't listen.''

"Couldn't you have put him off?''

"Could you have?''

He didn't respond. They both knew the answer to that one.

Jared growled low in his throat. "It's bad enough that he can't seem to trust me to run the business, but he also can't trust me to run my own life.''

"It's because he loves you and he doesn't know another way of showing it. Was he this way with your father?''

"Meddling? No. Dad wanted a career in medicine. He and mom were childhood sweethearts so Granddad always knew and liked her....'' He paused.

Brittnie glanced away as the heat of embarrassment swept through her. She knew he must be feeling the same thing as they both remembered that Roberto said Brittnie was like Miranda and Jared should marry her.

After a long, uncomfortable silence, Jared asked, "Where are we going to put him?''

When he asked that, Brittnie knew he'd finally accepted yet another instance of his grandfather's meddling.

"I don't know," she admitted. "There's still too much *stuff* in this house for it to hold so many people.''

"Especially one who's sick and shouldn't be here.''

Brittnie raised an eyebrow at him. Actually, there were two people who shouldn't be here, but she wasn't going to mention Linda. "I suppose we should stop acting as though someone is forcing us to store a box of dynamite under the bed and think of how to arrange things.''

Jared shook his head in defeat. "Any suggestions?''

It gave her a pang to realize that the obvious solution would be for Jared and his fiancée to share a room—not that Roberto would allow that. On the other hand, Jared hadn't seemed to want to do that, even when Linda first arrived.

"You'll have to let him use the room you're in," she said, slowly. "He can't climb the stairs to the second floor. His nurse will only be here during the day as a precaution. He says his doctor has told him he won't need medical attention at night."

"Unless I get my hands around his throat," Jared said darkly.

Brittnie snickered.

He looked up, his dark eyes narrowing. "You think this is funny?"

"No, sir, not me." The thunderous look on his face had her swiping away her grin, but it came right back, making her lips tremble and her eyes sparkle.

"You *do* think it's funny."

Brittnie had been sitting on the edge of the sofa but now she flopped back in a boneless sprawl, her head against a supporting cushion. She rolled her eyes and spoke to the ceiling, her voice full of laughter. "I think it's hilarious. Insane. You're threatening to strangle the grandfather whose health you're so worried about."

"Think of the savings in doctor's bills," he groused.

She broke up laughing.

"Hey, it wasn't that hilarious."

"The whole thing is. In fact, it's riotous. If this was a situation comedy on television, no one would believe it."

"*I* don't believe it and I'm living it." He glowered at her. "And you'd better quit laughing."

"I can't," she said, his expression sending her into

another fit of mirth. "It's too crazy. Who would have thought that a simple, straightforward job would turn out like this? I'm supposed to be sorting, classifying, and cataloging the belongings of a deceased attorney. First his brother comes to help me. That's fine, because he really is a help, but his grandson thinks I'm working the poor old guy too hard and not watching out for him."

Jared came to tower over her. "Now, wait a minute, I never said...."

She pointed a finger at him. "Oh, yes, you did."

"Well, maybe I did give a hint of my concerns," he said with mock pomposity.

"A hint?" She cleared her throat theatrically and threw her arms wide again, but she lowered her voice, aware of the woman upstairs. "Then the grandfather decides I'm just the girl to marry his grandson, but darned if the grandson doesn't already have a fiancée. No problem, the grandfather says, the grandson will just have to change his mind. Granddad works himself into a frazzle, ends up in the hospital, the grandson comes to stay with me, the fiancée follows, and now the grandfather. Does that about cover it?"

Brittnie looked up to meet his eyes as she asked the question. She was stretched out on the sofa, her dark blond hair in a tumble behind her, her long legs extended and crossed at the ankle, her arms thrown up and resting along the back of the sofa. Her attitude said she was welcoming his answer.

To her surprise, Jared came closer, placing his legs on each side of hers, encasing them. He leaned over, grasped her around the wrists, and brought her hands down to rest in her lap. Then he placed his hands on each side of her head and looked down into her eyes. She was caged in by him.

"Yeah," he said in a quiet tone that didn't match the devilish spark in his eyes. "That about covers it."

Brittnie's breath felt as if it had been corked in her throat. She could see flecks of gold in his eyes that she'd never seen before. She saw the thickness of his lashes that softened the firm lines of his face. She looked at his full, lower lip that had such a sensuous slant and remembered how devastating and how wonderful it was to kiss him.

Oh, no, she thought. *Here we go again.* But she didn't move away from him.

His gaze roamed over her flushed face. "So you think my family's hilarious, hmm?"

In spite of the excitement tingling along her skin, she managed to shrug nonchalantly. "You and Roberto are a laugh a minute. John and Miranda seem relatively normal." She chuckled again. "But then, I only met them recently, so I can't really tell yet."

Jared leaned closer, the intensity growing in his eyes. "Brittnie?"

"Yes, Jared?"

"It's rude to laugh at a man and his family."

She wrinkled her forehead as she considered it. "Well, technically, I was only laughing at part of it."

"Mostly me."

"True."

"It's rude, Brittnie."

She winced comically. "Damages the ego, does it?"

"Beyond repair." He moved in a bit more so that now his face filled her vision. "There's only one thing to do."

The humor was quickly draining out of this situation and danger was taking its place, sparking along Brittnie's nerve endings. Her budding headache had disappeared. It was being replaced by a different kind of ache; a pleasant, but risky one. Still she didn't back off. "What would that be?"

His eyes settled on her lips. "You've got to pay a forfeit."

"How much of one?"

His long, thick lashes swept down to hide his expression. "It may be more than you'd like to pay."

Brittnie angled her chin up the tiniest bit. The movement begged him to kiss her. "We won't know that," she said breathlessly. "Until you tell me what the forfeit is."

His dark eyes, full of teasing, came back up to meet hers. He leaned in, bringing his mouth to within a millimeter of hers. If she'd wanted to, she could have closed that gap, but he was making the moves here, so she let him.

"Brittnie, the forfeit is another piece of your mother's German chocolate cake."

Brittnie's mouth opened. She knew what she'd been expecting, and that hadn't been it. "Cake?" she wheezed.

She could tell he also knew what she'd been expecting and enjoyed teasing by not giving it to her. "Unless you've eaten it all?"

Affronted, she ducked away from him. "Of course not."

"Good." He stepped back, reached for her hands, and pulled her to her feet. "Let's go."

"Didn't you have dessert with dinner?" she asked, gently disentangling her fingers from his grip. It was definitely a bad idea for her to get accustomed to his touch. She already liked it far too much. Besides, she was still irritated with him for his teasing—at least she wanted to be.

"I didn't even have *dinner*," he said.

"Whyever not? I thought that's where you and Linda were headed."

"After we saw Granddad, I stopped by the office to get a few things done. She got tired of waiting for me and went off by herself for a while." He didn't sound upset by it. In fact, he sounded pleased. "It was the best thing for her to do."

"Oh, well, that's…fine," she answered, but she couldn't help recalling how upset they had both been when they had walked in. She speculated that Linda had been angry that his work had taken precedence over her.

Brittnie opened the refrigerator and began removing sandwich ingredients. Perversely, her heart insisted on being glad that he hadn't had dinner with Linda. "Here, help yourself."

"Thanks." He flipped the lid off a container of chicken salad, grabbed some bread and made himself a sandwich, then spied some roast beef and made a sandwich of that, too. While he ate, Brittnie cut the cake, put slices on two plates, grabbed a couple of forks, shut the drawer with a swing of her hips, and came to the table. She smiled as she sat down.

"What's funny this time?" Jared asked, taking a drink of milk and wiping his mouth with a napkin plucked from the holder on the table, a fifties-style pink plastic elephant who held the napkins in his upraised trunk.

"It's strange that with this huge house full of rooms and furniture, this is the place where we always seem to gravitate." She looked around the kitchen with its old-fashioned cast-iron sink, the glass-fronted cabinets holding a mix-and-match collection of Fiesta dishes which fought for space with a partial set of Wedgwood and several pieces of exquisite Spode china.

The range was a funky old thing with enameled metal covers that slid up from the back and covered the burners. The floor was old, too; clay-based linoleum with a pattern of red and black chevrons stamped into it. It was awful, but she liked it.

"That's because this is the most inviting room," he answered. "The others are still depressingly full of junk."

"Maybe." Brittnie shrugged. "It's the same way at home, at the ranch. We always end up in the kitchen."

"That's because of your mother's cooking, but I think it's that way everywhere," Jared said. "People like to be where the food is."

"I know I do," she agreed, sliding a plate to him, and turning hers so she could eat it, frosting first. She scooped some onto her fork. It was rich with pecans and coconut. She tasted it and let the buttery caramel flavor melt on her tongue.

He chuckled. "That's what I like about you, Brittnie. You enjoy simple pleasures."

As opposed to complicated ones like falling in love with him, she thought. She wasn't enjoying that at all.

"I'm just an old-fashioned girl, at heart," she answered flippantly.

"But you don't like to cook."

"I said 'at heart,' not 'in ability.'"

"You like this house, don't you?" he asked after a moment.

She looked up, tilting her head as she thought about it. "Yes, I guess I do. Some parts more than others. Of course, it needs to be renovated and redecorated from basement to attic, but it could be very livable. And with the right cook and housekeeper, it would be perfect.''

He laughed at that as he slid his dessert plate over and began demolishing his slice of cake.

''It would be nice to live here, in the historic district, it gives a sense of...permanency,'' she went on as she contemplated a bite of the coconut and pecan frosting. ''This house needs a family in it. Perhaps you and Linda should live here after you're married.''

She didn't know why she'd added that last part except that her heart seemed to stubbornly harbor hopes of hearing him deny that he and Linda would marry. Brittnie knew better than that. If he had made a promise, he would stick to it.

Jared rested his fork against the edge of his plate. He didn't look up as he said, ''No. This isn't the kind of house Linda would like to live in.''

''Oh,'' she said, knowing it was the most inadequate of responses. ''What about you? Would you like a house like this—at least until you're married?''

''I have a condo. It meets my needs.''

''That didn't really answer my question.''

He met her gently questioning smile. ''Yes,'' he said gruffly. ''I've always liked this place, although when I was a kid, I thought it was haunted, that my uncle lived with ghosts.''

''I thought the same thing the first time I walked in here.''

''In a way, he did,'' Jared said. ''He wasn't a happy man. He seemed driven, somehow, and yet closed off, as if something was eating at him, but we never knew what it was.''

''Even Roberto says he never really knew him,'' Brittnie agreed.

"Yes, and I think it's bothered Granddad more since he's gotten older, especially since Uncle David died." He paused and finished his cake before continuing. "They couldn't even spend their retirement years together because neither of them wanted to retire. Uncle David always seem to have responsibilities pushing him."

"What kind of responsibilities?"

"Toward people. Until he was ninety, he still maintained an office and went in every day, though most of his cases were *pro bono*. He didn't always charge people because he said he had more money than he'd be able to spend in his lifetime. As it turned out, he was right."

"And then he came home every day to this jam-packed house," Brittnie said sadly.

"I don't think he really noticed it. Granddad says he lived mostly in his bedroom, the library, and the kitchen."

Brittnie smiled. "Back to the kitchen."

Jared was silent, his lean face drawn into a frown. It seemed to be directed inward rather than at her, so she went on. "Why didn't your uncle use the downstairs bedroom, Jared? I would have thought it would be easier for him than climbing the stairs."

"I don't know except that he said that upstairs room had been his for forty years and he didn't intend to change."

She grinned. "Couldn't be that famous Cruz stubbornness, could it?"

"Nah. Couldn't be." He smiled, too, then let it fade as he contemplated her. She gave him a puzzled look.

"Is something wrong?"

"I think I need to tell you something about my family, Brittnie."

"Go on," she prompted.

Jared took a breath. "Granddad started his own business after World War II. He'd run the farm before the war, but he wasn't interested in farming afterward, so he and David sold it when their parents died. He started out as a night watchman, then as a caretaker. Later, he became a property manager. His business grew because he was a man who fulfilled his responsibilities. People knew they could count on him."

Brittnie laid her fork quietly on her plate, her appetite gone. She wasn't sure where this was heading, but something in his tone told her it was important and she might not like where it ended.

"My dad didn't want to be in the family business. He liked medicine. He could have gone into research but he wanted to work with patients. He's tried hard to never let any of them down."

"That's...commendable," Brittnie said.

"That's my legacy, Brittnie. I come from a long line of men who fulfill their responsibilities." His eyes had gone midnight black and were full of urgency. He leaned forward and laid his hand over hers. Turning it, he held it tightly.

Brittnie felt a shock run through her, not only from his touch, but because of the look in his eyes as if he desperately wanted her to understand what he was telling her. Her other hand came up to grasp his. "Yes. You told me that before, but I don't understand what you're saying, Jared."

"That you're an attractive woman, Brittnie. You're smart and strong and persistent."

"And is that good or bad?" she asked uncertainly. She couldn't imagine where this was leading, but hope and dread tugged at her simultaneously.

"It's good." He shook his head. "I wish it wasn't, but it's good."

"Thank you, I guess," she said, barely able to choke the words out.

"But I'm also saying that I never should have touched you. Never should have kissed you." His voice was low and urgent. Brittnie had to lean close to hear the rest of what he was saying. She saw emotions working in his face and none of them seemed to be happy ones. "There's something about you—many things about you—your vitality, energy, your brains that attract me to you."

"You don't...don't sound happy about it."

"I'm not, damn it. I'm responsible for...."

"Jared?"

The hesitant voice from the doorway had them springing apart as if they'd been caught in some illicit act. Brittnie was so startled, she whipped around in her chair, eyes guilty, face flushed.

Linda stood in the doorway, dressed in a navy blue silk robe, her bright hair spilling around her face, her own eyes wide with shock. "What are you doing?"

Jared gave Brittnie a quick look. In it, she thought she read a plea for understanding, but she didn't know what he was asking her to understand. She looked from him to Linda, and back again, begging for some kind of explanation.

It didn't come. He stood smoothly and crossed the room. "We were having a snack," he said. "I'm sorry if we woke you."

"You didn't, but...." She glanced back at Brittnie who was frozen in place. "Jared, it looked like you were holding her hand."

"I was," he said honestly, as he put his arm around

her shoulder and hurried her out the door. The remainder of his reply was lost as it closed behind them.

Brittnie sat staring after them. Yes, he had been holding her hand, explaining that he shouldn't have kissed her, but he was attracted to her. Surely, he wasn't going to tell Linda that. His sense of responsibility certainly couldn't be *that* strong! But what was he going to say? That it meant nothing? Brittnie meant nothing? She didn't think that was true, but how could she know?

She propped her elbows on the table, and rested her head in her hands, pressing the heels against her eyes in hopes of holding back tears. This wasn't fair, she thought furiously. It wasn't fair that she had fallen in love with a man who found her attractive, but couldn't love her. And it really wasn't fair that he had ever touched her when there was another woman in his life. Deep in her heart, that was what bothered her the most because she couldn't match up the conscientious, honorable man she knew with someone who would do such a thing.

Upset and confused, she stood and cleared their things from the table, shakily tossing out the remainder of her dessert and washing the plates. She should be glad, she thought hysterically, that he at least accepted responsibility for kissing her, touching her, finding her attractive and vital.

Too bad, she couldn't blame him for making her fall in love with him, but that was strictly her own folly.

A full stomach and a troubled conscience didn't make for a restful night. Brittnie woke, groggy and grumpy, and sat on the side of her bed, feet resting on the floor. She didn't want to get up, to go downstairs, to face Linda Pomfort, or worst of all, Jared. She didn't want him to finish what he'd started to say last night, to hear about his regrets.

Right now, she wanted to go out to her mother's ranch and take her horse, Misty, for a ride. She wanted to run as hard as possible across the fields and up into the San Juans, to blow the problems and the pressures from her mind.

She couldn't, though, because there was work to do. Her second choice would be to close herself off somewhere, and do her job, avoiding contact with Jared, Linda, and Roberto when he showed up again. She knew that was unreasonable, though. Since the job would take many more months yet, there was no way she could avoid seeing them unless she locked herself in this room.

Not an option, she thought, pushing herself off the bed and heading for the shower. Half an hour later, she started downstairs, passing the room Linda was using. The door was closed, indicating that she was still asleep. No wonder. Brittnie had heard Linda and Jared's voices coming from that room for a long time after he had led the distressed girl from the kitchen. He had left, though, far past midnight, and that's when Brittnie had thankfully fallen asleep.

Brittnie wasn't going to be a hypocrite. She'd been relieved that Jared hadn't spent the night with Linda.

She ran her hand along the banister as she descended the stairs. Last night she'd thought the situation was humorous, but this morning she couldn't even dredge up a smile, much less a laugh.

Thinking of her favorite pecan-flavored coffee, piping hot, Brittnie pushed open the door to the kitchen and found that it was already occupied. Linda sat at the table, sipping from a mug. She looked up when Brittnie came in.

"Good morning."

Brittnie recovered herself. "Good morning." She strode in, took a coffee mug from the shelf and poured it full. The scent of the fragrant brew filled the room. Brittnie took a sip and looked at Linda with new respect. At least she could make coffee. She complimented Linda on it, and received a hesitant nod in return. Brittnie made herself some toast and brought it to the table along with a jar of orange marmalade. She didn't know quite why she was so intent on striving for normalcy in the face of this situation, but somehow it seemed to salve her pride.

She would have preferred to be by herself, but her parents had drilled manners into her and Brittnie could think of no reason to rudely take her breakfast to another part of the house.

As Brittnie looked down at her toast and coffee, she tried to think of a time in her life when she had been more uncomfortable. The only one she could think of was when Steve had followed her into the elevator in Jared's building—but Jared had rescued her.

There would be no rescue from him today. Or if there was, she knew she wouldn't be the one to be rescued by him. Where was he, anyway? she wondered.

Linda set down her coffee and cleared her throat. She laced her fingers together and placed her hands on top of the table as she gave Brittnie a steady look. "Jared explained about last night."

"He did?" Dread settled in Brittnie's stomach. She cut her toast into squares and carefully spread each one with marmalade. She was quite proud of the steadiness of her hands. "What did he say?"

"That you've become good friends, but you're still...only an employee."

Fury with him lapped at Brittnie. "Is that right?" she asked in a tight voice.

Linda gave another of her superior looks, her beautiful face stiff with purpose, her lips drawn together. "He's attracted to you, but I know I have nothing to worry about."

Alternate waves of anger and embarrassment ran through Brittnie, but she was determined to keep her cool. "I see," she said through her teeth.

"Jared's always taken care of me," Linda continued. Her voice shook and she covered it by clearing her throat. "He'll always be there for me. That's what he said."

"He wouldn't lie to you," Brittnie said, but she wondered why he had lied to *her* by his actions, his demonstrations of affection and desire. "And he always fulfills his responsibilities."

Linda nodded. "That's what he told me. That's why I know I can always depend on him. When…when we're married, I won't have to worry that he'll…he'll abandon me…." Her voice trailed off and her self-assured attitude began to crumple. Her throat worked spasmodically as if she was fighting for control. "He loves me."

"I'm sure he does," Brittnie answered, though the words caught in her throat.

Linda gripped her mug with trembling hands. The tips of her fingers were white. "He doesn't love you."

Pain shot through Brittnie as if she had been stabbed. "No," she said. "He doesn't." It nearly killed her to speak the truth.

"He just met you. He doesn't even know you. Even when we saw you in that restaurant, I…I knew right away that he was attracted to you, but…attraction doesn't mean love."

Brittnie wanted to run, wanted to be sick, get out of this room, but she was frozen in place. Her hands gripped the edge of the table, her back was as stiff as a freshly sawn board. She felt as if her insides were breaking into tiny pieces.

"He loves me," Linda said again. "He's always taken care of me."

"I...I know," Brittnie choked. She watched the other girl through the tears that were pooling in her eyes.

Linda stood suddenly. Brittnie would have expected her to look triumphant, but instead, she seemed nervous and looked ill at ease. "I've got to go," she said, her gaze darting around the room, looking everywhere but at Brittnie. "I'm supposed to visit my mother today."

In spite of her own pain, Brittnie noticed that Linda was wearing a dark green suit, cut on severe lines. It made her wonder what kind of relationship the girl had with her mother that required business attire. Then she recalled what Shannon had said about Linda's family, and pity surfaced through her pain.

As Linda hurried out, Brittnie sat at the same table where she'd sat last night and finally let the tears run down her cheeks. Linda said Jared had always taken care of her, that he loved her, would marry her.

Brittnie knew that. He'd said as much himself. And she knew he didn't lie.

CHAPTER TEN

BRITTNIE knew she needed to move, to get up and do something, but she couldn't seem to get her arms and legs to obey her. Even her hands couldn't pick up a napkin to wipe away her tears.

She knew it was only the physical effects of the emotional blow she'd experienced, but she felt as if she had been struck with a type of flu. It had turned her muscles to water and her bones to rubber. The best thing she could do was sit for a while until she pulled herself together.

She still hadn't managed to move when she heard the front door close, telling her that Linda had left. Relieved, Brittnie got to her feet, steadied herself against the edge of the table, then shuffled to the sink. She tossed her forgotten toast in the trash and poured her coffee down the drain. It seemed she had found a cure for her hearty appetite.

She started when she heard the back door slam. She turned around to see Jared coming into the kitchen. He was dressed in shorts, T-shirt, and running shoes. Even though the morning was cool, perspiration glistened on his skin and dampened his hair, telling her that he'd been running for a long time.

She hadn't known that he was a runner, but it explained how he kept in shape in spite of his desk job.

Brittnie had never found sweating men to be attractive. She thought it was because she'd been around so many of them growing up on the ranch. When Jared walked in, though, she felt the impact of his maleness roll across the room and punch her in the stomach. His appearance was such a contrast from his usual impeccable dress—and so disturbing.

A small towel hung around his neck. He whipped it off and blotted sweat from his face before he glanced up and saw her.

His gaze swept over her and stopped at her stricken face. "Brittnie, what's wrong?" He took a step forward, but she retreated.

"Nothing," she lied. Glad that some life was flowing back into her limbs, she spun around and headed for the door. "Linda has gone out, in case you were wondering where she is, and...." She let her words trail off as she left the room. She didn't know what else she had planned to say, anyway. The heck with it. Let him worry about his fiancée. It wasn't her concern.

He came after her, catching the swinging door as it came toward him and stalking behind her through the dining room. "I wasn't wondering. I knew she would be gone...I...encouraged her to visit her mother today...Brittnie stop. I want to talk to you."

She lifted her chin as she glanced at him over her shoulder. "There's no need."

He gave her an incredulous stare. "Yes, there is. I want to explain about last night, finish what I was trying to say before...."

"Before your fiancée caught us holding hands?" Brittnie fought to cut the bitterness from her tone as she sailed into the entryway, but she wasn't completely successful. It seeped out anyway and made her voice crack. "I told you, there's no need to talk about it."

"Damn it, will you slow down?"

"No, I won't," she shot back, but she paused with

one foot on the first tread of the staircase and her hand on the newel post. "I already know what you were trying to tell me last night."

He stopped and put his hands on his hips. "You must be clairvoyant, then, because I never finished what I wanted to say."

"You were going to say that you accept responsibility for...." Her voice faltered, but she forced herself to go on. "For kissing me, for being attracted to me when you're engaged to Linda. That it's wrong."

His jaw thrust out and his eyes narrowed. "That's not what...."

"Or words to that effect," she broke in. "This isn't entirely your fault. I accept the responsibility, too. We're both adults. We were carried away by proximity, by a sudden need to be close to someone else...."

"In other words, 'this thing is bigger than both of us,' is that it?"

She ignored his sardonic tone and plowed ahead. "We made a mistake, one that won't be repeated. Our only relationship is strictly professional, not personal. It will never be personal."

His hands fisted and punched into the air. "There you go again with that dam-burst of words. You don't know what the hell you're talking about because you won't give me a chance to explain."

"You don't owe me any explanations," she said with dignity. "You don't owe me anything. Excuse me, Jared, but I have work to do." She spun on her toe and started trotting up the stairs.

Behind her, he growled in frustration. "Then I won't explain," he called after her. "Why would I bother talking to someone who knows everything, anyway? It would be a waste of time!" The last words were shouted as she reached the landing and streaked down the hall-way to her room.

She whirled inside and slammed the door, then took a few agitated turns around the room before collapsing in a slump on the side of the bed. This had been a terrible mistake. All her talk about being a professional, about doing the best job possible, had been a lie. She wasn't behaving in a professional manner at all. She had convinced Jared to let her live in the house because she'd thought it would be beneficial to be on site, but all she'd managed to do was to get herself deeply entrenched in Cruz family affairs, fall in love with Jared, and make a fool of herself.

That was going to stop. She would leave right now. The job be hanged. David's missing journal be hanged, she thought hysterically. Let Jared and Linda look for it. She was going home to the Kelleher ranch and hide out.

Miss Brittnie Kelleher was finally going to develop a few smarts and get out of this place. Leaping up, she rushed to the closet and pulled out her suitcases. She slammed them onto the bed and whipped them open, then scurried to the high chest to scoop clothing from the drawers.

In her haste, she caught a slip strap on the front corner of a drawer. Trying to free it, she jerked and was horrified to see the entire front fall away. It clattered to the floor as she made a grab for it. She only succeeded in redirecting its fall so that it barked up against her shin.

She grunted in pain, tossed the armful of clothing onto the bed, and bent to retrieve the drawer front, berating herself for wrecking the furniture. She would have to repair it before she left, delaying her departure from the house.

As she picked up the piece of carved wood by the

handle, she saw that it had been attached by small finishing nails which had pulled straight out of the drawer.
She laid it on top of the chest, then reached for the empty
drawer. As she pulled it out, she caught sight of something dull green. Puzzled, she leaned closer and was
astonished to see that the drawer had a false bottom.
Between it and the real drawer bottom was a narrow
compartment. It was exactly the right size to fit David
Cruz's missing journal, which rested inside.

Her heart beating at a light, rapid pace, Brittnie
worked her fingers into the opening and withdrew the
small book. A dozen questions flew through her mind
as she flipped it open.

Immediately, she saw that this volume was different.
It was dated two months after the end of the last journal.
It wasn't cross-written and it had only a few entries.
Reading rapidly, Brittnie made her way back to the bed
and sank down, absently shoving aside the pile of cloth-
ing.

She read of the culmination of David's agonies in the
war, of his terror when German shells screamed and
burst overhead, then his helplessness as his friends
screamed and died around him. Months, and then years
of such terrors had taken their toll. The survivor's guilt
was more than he could bear.

The journal entries Brittnie had read before were often
written in short, choppy sentences, as if David had
seemed to be in a hurry, or in precise prose. This one
rambled, often making no sense so that she had to reread
an entry several times to understand it.

After one battle, when he had lain all night in knee-
deep water, beside the bodies of his friends, he had
snapped. David Cruz, reliable farmboy from Colorado,
volunteer hoping to cover himself with glory in a war

that wasn't even his own, had broken and run when his position was overrun by the enemy. He had left his dead friends behind, climbed out of the trench, and deserted.

The journal ended there. Weak with shock, Brittnie let it fall shut in her lap, then she sat and stared at it as she wondered how she was going to tell Roberto. How could she tell him anything? He would be terribly upset and the shock might make him sick again. Brittnie reminded herself that she had just been thinking that she had become too involved in the Cruz family affairs. Roberto's reaction wasn't for her to decide, but before giving the volume to him, she needed to talk to Jared.

Her own distress forgotten, she left her room and hurried downstairs where she found Jared in the kitchen. He was fresh from a shower, his hair still damp and tousled carelessly by a towel. He wore jeans and a black T-shirt and was pouring himself a cup of coffee.

"Back for round two?" he asked sardonically as she walked in, but his face went blank with surprise when he saw how upset she was. "What is it? What's wrong?" he asked, sliding the cup onto the counter and hurrying over to her.

"I found it." She held up the journal and told him where it had turned up. With stumbling apologies for giving him bad news, she told him what she'd read.

"Come on," he said, taking it from her hand and leading her from the kitchen. When they reached the living room, he made her sit down on the sofa, then he reached down and scooped her feet up and onto the coffee table. "You've had a shock."

He sat down beside her and gripped her hand in his. This time, she didn't think about the rightness or wrongness of it. They both needed comfort.

Her eyes swam with sympathetic tears as she looked

at him. "No, I've only had an unhappy surprise. This must be a shock to you because he's your uncle and...."

"I knew him as an old man, Brittnie," Jared said, opening the journal. "Remember, he was ninety-five when he died. You're the one who's been reading these journals, so you've come to know him as a scared kid. That makes it much more personal."

Touched by his sensitivity, Brittnie nodded. "Maybe so. I'm puzzled, though, because I found his discharge papers. I gave them to your grandfather. They looked genuine, and besides, if he'd been a deserter, the family would have known."

Jared nodded. "The whole community would have known. No, David must have gone back before anyone discovered he'd deserted, or maybe his superiors thought he'd become separated from his unit in the confusion of battle."

"Why did he stop writing in his journal, then? Why did he even keep the journal?"

"Brittnie, look around you. David kept everything. He couldn't seem to get rid of items the way most people do—even something as painful as this," Jared answered, lifting the slim volume. "It didn't make any sense, but he seemed to have been emotionally attached to it somehow."

"I guess you're right, but why did he hide it away and refuse to talk about the war at all for the rest of his life—not even to Roberto?"

"Shame." Jared's eyes were dark and troubled. "He'd run away, shucked off his responsibility, and even though he came back later, he was traumatized by what he'd done." He paused, looking thoughtful. "And he spent the rest of his life trying to make up for it by helping people through his law practice."

"Yes." Brittnie gripped his fingers, drawing strength from him. "It...helps to think of it like that, but it seems sad that he let that blight the rest of his life—at least his relationships with people, especially with his own brother."

"Remember, Granddad was just a little kid at that time. He hero-worshipped David."

"You're right, of course. I just don't understand why he had to hide it."

"Brittnie, don't you get it?" Jared asked gently. "It's that Cruz stubbornness and overdeveloped sense of responsibility that I was telling you about last night."

Her lips trembling, she met his eyes again, and then glanced away. She didn't want to get back on that subject. Instead, she said, "I don't know what we're going to tell Roberto. This might be too much of a shock for him."

"I'll handle it," Jared answered. "I'll talk to my dad about it."

"I'm sure that's best," she said shakily. Aware of the intimacy of their position, side by side, hands clasped, Brittnie moved away. She cleared her throat as she stood. "I guess that solves the mystery." She clasped her hands at her waist and looked down at the way she had twisted her fingers together. She was really beginning to perfect this handwringing thing. "Now that we've found this, there's no reason for you to stay."

"Kicking me out of my own house, Brittnie?" He tossed the journal on the table and rose to stand before her.

"It's best if you leave, Jared. You hired me to do this job and I need to be left alone to do it," she rambled, completely forgetting that half an hour earlier she had been packing her own bags.

His expression was harsh as he looked into her face. "I think leaving you alone would be the worst thing to do. I left you alone last night and you got up this morning refusing to listen to me."

She met his eyes. "Jared, there's nothing to say. You don't owe me any explanations. Those need to go to your fiancée."

Jared opened his mouth to answer, then snapped it shut again. There was nothing to say, and they both knew it. His hands came up as if to grip her shoulders, but Brittnie gave him such a look of alarm, he cursed under his breath.

"Hell, don't look at me like I'm going to attack you."

She ran shaky hands through her hair. "It's best if you don't touch me, don't…make me want you to touch me." Fraud, her conscience prodded her. She only had to be in the same room with him in order to want his touch. His love.

The look he gave her was long and hard, then she saw a flicker of regret which was quickly hidden. He walked to the doorway, paused, and spoke to her without turning around. "You're right, of course. At least finding the journal puts an end to Granddad's plan to move in. I'll get my things out, and Linda will, too. This morning."

Brittnie swallowed the lump forming in her throat. "Fine. I'll continue on here, and…." She paused, trying to form words to say what she didn't want to say. "Jared, if you need to contact me, why don't you have Sandra call?"

That brought him around to face her again. His eyes snapped and his jaw worked as if he wanted to argue, but the tears standing in her eyes and the set of her trembling chin must have told him she couldn't take much more. "All right." He turned away, only to stop in the doorway. He extended both arms out until his hands gripped the sides of the opening. His head drooped in dejection, then he dropped his hands and walked away.

Brittnie stared after him with tears spilling from her eyes. If she didn't know better, she would think he was as devastated by this as she was, felt the same pain and loss. But she knew better. If he felt it, he didn't show it. He had other responsibilities, or at least one—Linda—and she came first.

Brittnie stood the silence and loneliness of the house for a full week before she reached her limit. It was too quiet—even the most fanatic librarian wouldn't want this much quiet. She worked steadily, sorting, cataloging, making arrangements with the historical society to receive items significant to the history of the area. Though constantly busy, she still found that she had far too much time to think.

She convinced herself that her heart wasn't broken. Jared hadn't made any promises to her that he had later broken. He hadn't forced her to fall in love with him. It had happened, she was responsible, and she would deal with it.

She arrived at these lofty conclusions late every evening, enabling her to sleep, and woke each morning with the depressing knowledge that she was a fraud and it would take a very long time to get over Jared.

Her mood alarmed her family and Shannon was delegated to do whatever was necessary to find out what was wrong. Brittnie didn't want to confess her foolishness, but she couldn't resist her sister's persistence, so she finally told all. Shannon hugged her while she cried, handed her tissues to wipe her eyes, then, ever practical, reminded her that she could either wallow in self-pity or move ahead with her life. Brittnie knew this advice wasn't new or original, but it helped to hear it from someone who loved her.

Roberto called to thank her for finding the last journal. He said Jared had prepared him for it ahead of time, so the shock wasn't too great, but discovering the fact of his brother's desertion had clarified much that he'd never understood about David. He told her about his plans to recuperate at home, then go to Arizona for the winter.

Before he hung up, he said, "Have you seen that grandson of mine lately?"

Brittnie's heart thumped into her stomach. Simply hearing about Jared was disturbing. "No," she said after a moment. "Sandra has been handling everything to do with my job. I'm sure he's been busy."

"So he says. He looks like hell."

Brittnie, standing in the kitchen, glanced at her own reflection in the glass front of a cabinet. So did she. "I'm sorry to hear that," she murmured.

"I'm sorry, too," Roberto said gruffly. "I'm sorry that things didn't work out between you two."

"Roberto," she answered in a gentle tone. "There was never anything to work out."

"Pull the other one, honey. You two are right for each other. You could keep him from being such a damned serious workaholic, and he could keep your feet on the ground."

Brittnie shoved a shaky hand through her tumbled hair. Yes, that was exactly what they could have done for each other.

When she didn't answer, Roberto sighed, said he'd be in touch again soon, and hung up.

Brittnie replaced the receiver slowly, took one look

around the empty, echoing kitchen, and decided she needed a day off. She would go to the ranch, saddle Misty, and go for a long ride.

When she arrived at the ranch, she avoided the house, and contact with any member of her family and went straight to the storage shed where she had stored her things. She dug out her boots. Even though it was the middle of October, the day was warm enough that she wouldn't need a jacket. She located a hat that had belonged to her father, brushed the dust off of it, and put it on.

Brittnie found her saddle in the tack room, then went out to the pasture to catch Misty, a big roan who ran with a surprisingly light pacing stride. Misty cantered up and nipped at Brittnie's hair, making her laugh. Immediately, she felt better. She should have done this days ago. Misty was as ready for a hard run as Brittnie was.

When she had the mare saddled, she headed out of the corral and across the yard. She saw her mother's ranch hand, Lenny Branscom, trot up on horseback and she waved as she rode away, glad that she had escaped talking to anyone. She rode across the pasture and into the foothills that backed up against the ranch. There was a small valley a few miles away which had been her special place since she had first learned to ride. She dug her boot heels into Misty's sides, and the mare leaped ahead, stretching out into a full run. Within minutes, they had skirted the boundary between the Kelleher ranch and the one belonging to Gus Blackhawk. Brittnie was careful not to stray onto his land. He was a sour old man who didn't like anybody, especially the Kellehers, and nothing would make him happier than to bring charges against one of them for trespassing.

Brittnie pulled back on the reins, slowing Misty, then urging her to climb the slope that made a path to her valley. She couldn't wait to get there, to turn Misty loose to graze, while she sat with her back against a rock and her eyes on the horizon. She didn't plan to do any serious thinking, she'd done enough of that already and it hadn't solved anything except to make her feel depressed and to worry her family.

When she heard another horse behind her, she looked over her shoulder, hoping it wasn't her mother riding out to check on her.

It was a man.

With an irritated sound, Brittnie turned back. If Mr. Blackhawk had seen her pass and had sent a ranch hand to harass her, both men were going to get an earful. She spurred Misty and her powerful legs churned as she climbed the slope. When they reached the top, she glanced back to see that the man was still coming.

From her vantage point, she could get a better look at him and was surprised to see that he was bareheaded. His dark hair looked black in the bright sun. When he lifted his head to gauge her distance from him, she saw with a shock that it was Jared.

Brittnie closed her eyes, convinced she was seeing things, then opened them again. Jared was directing his horse to follow hers, urging it to take the slope. Another shock zipped through her when she realized that the horse was the one Lenny had been riding.

In a moment of blind panic, Brittnie tugged on the reins, spinning Misty around and sending her in a dash down the wide, shallow slope to the valley.

She heard Jared call out, but she didn't stop. Instead, she raced across the valley. There was nowhere to go, though, except to circle the area and come back, which she did with Jared pounding along behind her. After a few minutes, she realized she was being foolish—just as she had been the first day they'd met when she'd been running and hiding from Steve. She pulled up on the reins, stopping Misty, who danced a few steps, then settled down, her sides heaving.

Her hand on the reins, she urged Misty around, then she sat and waited for Jared.

He was beside her in seconds. "What was that all about?" he asked, pulling his own horse up so that they were side by side, facing each other.

"I don't know. I thought...." She shrugged helplessly. "I don't know what I thought. Jared, why are you here?"

"Well, obviously, to talk to you," he answered hotly. "I've been missing you by about five minutes all day. When I couldn't find you at the house, I decided to try your mother's ranch. Some guy named Lenny said he'd seen you come out here, so he let me borrow his horse."

For the first time, Brittnie focused on his clothes. He wasn't dressed like any horseman she'd ever seen, in brown dress slacks and a white shirt. No doubt, he'd left his tie and suit jacket in his car. She hadn't even known he could ride.

Brittnie brought stunned eyes up to meet his. "I can't imagine why he would have done that...."

"Because I told him I'm in love with you and I want to marry you."

Her mouth opened, but no words came out. She closed it and tried again. "What?"

A smile twitched at his lips. "I think you heard me."

"I...I guess I did, but I don't know what you mean. What about Linda?"

His smile faded. "I'd better explain about her." He

glanced around. "Is there someplace we can sit? Beneath those cedar trees, maybe?" He pointed to a small stand of them a few hundred yards away.

Brittnie nodded, turned, and walked her horse there while a thousand questions buzzed through her mind. When they reached the trees, they dismounted, left the horses to graze, and sat with their backs to a rock. The cedars' spiky branches arched over them, shielding them from the sun.

Brittnie searched Jared's face. He looked different than he had the last time she'd seen him a week ago, his expression open and at ease, his eyes fixed on her face.

"I wanted to explain about Linda weeks ago, Brittnie, but her secrets weren't mine to tell." He paused, as if forming his words carefully. "I've known her for several years. Her father owned a couple of office buildings that were the first ones Granddad let me manage on my own. She and I became friends but I saw right away that she was emotionally…needy."

Brittnie had seen that for herself.

"She never got much attention from her parents. They're self-absorbed. They seemed to be gone on a vacation whenever anything important was going on in her life." He took a deep breath. "Anyway, about a year and a half ago, she met a man she was crazy about. They talked about marriage, but then he broke it off."

Brittnie recalled Linda's statement that Jared would always take care of her. Now she knew why. No doubt, she'd been cared for all her life, but by servants and employees, not by people who truly loved her. "She must have been devastated."

"Worse than that." Jared looked up, his eyes full of sorrow. "She attempted suicide."

"Oh, Jared." Reaching out, Brittnie took his hand. She recalled that Shannon had told her Linda had been ill. It had been far more than illness.

"Her parents were out of the country and even then, they didn't get back for five days. I took care of her, she came to lean heavily on me. I couldn't abandon her. Everyone had abandoned her. She needed me. She started talking about marriage. I knew she didn't love me, and that marriage wasn't what she needed. I was willing to take care of her until she could stand on her own. She depended on me." His smile formed slowly. "And that was all right until a few weeks ago when a tall blonde whirled onto the elevator and announced that I was the new man in her life."

Brittnie smiled ruefully as heat climbed her cheeks.

"Don't be embarrassed," he laughed. "I was flattered, especially since I didn't know who in the world you were. From that moment, I wanted to know you, to pursue you, but Linda still depended on me."

"She told me you'd always take care of her."

"And I will," he answered seriously. "Whenever she needs me, I'll help her, but it's not going to be like it's been this past year. I've been trying to get her to visit her parents more, develop an adult relationship with them. She's been in counseling, but she hasn't made much progress. She didn't want to make the effort to help herself. She and I have had frequent discussions about it lately, arguments, even, but I saw that as a positive sign. At least she was willing to fight rather than meekly go along with whatever I said. She came to me this morning, and said that, at her counselor's suggestion, she's moving to Denver, that she's going to stop clinging to me and give me some breathing room. She told me that she panicked when I moved into Uncle David's house with you.''

"Why?"

"She'd seen that I couldn't take my eyes off of you when we met that night at the restaurant in Durango. Linda said if looks could have killed, the guy you were with would have been writhing on the floor.''

Brittnie recalled Linda's odd comment about Brittnie "knowing her boundaries.'' It made sense now in light of what Jared was telling her. Suddenly, she brightened. ''You were jealous?''

"Don't look so pleased,'' he growled.

"I'm just surprised,'' she said demurely, but her eyes laughed at him.

"Humph, I know how to fix your wagon, Miss Kelleher.'' He put his arms around her and spun her so that she lay across his lap.

"Oh!'' Her arms shot up to steady herself, and lingered to clasp at the back of his neck.

He lowered his head until his mouth was on hers. Slowly, reverently, they savored their first kiss that was unmarred by guilt. Brittnie's lips trembled against his and she pulled away. Resting her head against his chest, she whispered, ''I love you.''

Jared chuckled. ''I know, but Linda was the one who told me. This morning she said that when she saw me with you, she knew she didn't love me the way you do.''

"I must have been pretty obvious.''

"Not to me. She told me she'd tried to warn you off, but it made her realize she had become a person she doesn't want to be—weak and dependent. I hoped she was right about you loving me, but after I talked to her this morning, I started after you with shaking knees because I was afraid she had misread you.''

Brittnie kissed him again, weak with relief and full of joy. "She read me right. I've been in love with you since the day Roberto got sick and we were together in the hospital waiting room."

"If you agree to marry me, he's going to take credit for it."

"I will marry you, and I don't care who gets the credit as long as I get you."

They sat for a few more minutes as they made plans. Finally Jared pulled away. "We'd better get back. The guy who loaned me this horse probably told your mother what I said, and she'll be wondering what's happening."

"I think she probably knows," Brittnie said, sitting up and looking around for her hat. She whistled for Misty, who trotted up, followed by the horse Jared had ridden.

"What about Thanksgiving for our wedding? Remember. Granddad says it would be perfect."

"He's been hearing wedding bells since the day you and I met," Brittnie laughed. "But if he says we need a Thanksgiving wedding, then that's what we'd better have." She slid her hands around his waist and kissed him again. "Maybe it will help avoid any more of his meddling."

Jared groaned. "Don't count on it."

"I have a plan for Roberto," Brittnie announced, giving him one more hug, then standing to catch Misty's reins.

"Oh? What?"

"Do you remember when I told you about my great-aunt Katrina? The librarian?"

"Yes. What about her?"

"She's a beautiful woman in her seventies who looks twenty years younger than she is. She attributes it to having had many husbands and lovers. She's currently between husbands. I thought I'd send her Roberto's way."

Jared looked at her with admiration as he shoved his foot into the stirrup and climbed into the saddle. "That's why I love you. You're smart and sneaky when necessary, and...."

"And?" Brittnie looked up curiously as she mounted the mare.

Jared tugged the reins so his horse came up alongside hers. Bending to her, he gave Brittnie a light kiss. "And you say the damnedest things in elevators."

PENNY JORDAN,

DAY LECLAIRE &
LINDSAY ARMSTRONG

bring you the best of Christmas romance
in this wonderful holiday collection where
friends and family gather to celebrate
the holidays and make romantic wishes
come true.

Christmas Treats is available in November 1998,
at your favorite retail store.

◆ HARLEQUIN®
Makes any time special ™

Take 2 bestselling love stories FREE

Plus get a FREE surprise gift!

Special Limited-Time Offer

Mail to Harlequin Reader Service®

3010 Walden Avenue
P.O. Box 1867
Buffalo, N.Y. 14240-1867

YES! Please send me 2 free Harlequin Romance® novels and my free surprise gift. Then send me 6 brand-new novels every month, which I will receive months before they appear in bookstores. Bill me at the low price of $2.90 each plus 25¢ delivery and applicable sales tax if any*. That's the complete price, and a saving of over 10% off the cover prices—quite a bargain! I understand that accepting the books and gift places me under no obligation ever to buy any books. I can always return a shipment and cancel at any time. Even if I never buy another book from Harlequin, the 2 free books and the surprise gift are mine to keep forever.

116 HEN CH66

Name	(PLEASE PRINT)
Address	Apt. No.
City	State	Zip

This offer is limited to one order per household and not valid to present Harlequin Romance® subscribers. *Terms and prices are subject to change without notice. Sales tax applicable in N.Y.

UROM-98   ©1990 Harlequin Enterprises Limited

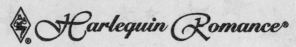

Remember the magic of the film
It's a Wonderful Life?
The warmth and tender emotion of
Truly, Madly, Deeply?
The feel-good humor of *Heaven Can Wait?*

Well, even if we can't promise you angels that look like Alan Rickman or Warren Beatty, starting in June in Harlequin Romance®, we can promise a brand-new miniseries: GUARDIAN ANGELS. Featuring all of your favorite ingredients for a perfect novel: great heroes, feisty heroines and a breathtaking romance—all with a celestial spin.

Look for Guardian Angels in:

June 1998: THE BOSS, THE BABY AND THE BRIDE (#3508)
by Day Leclaire

August 1998: HEAVENLY HUSBAND (#3516)
by Carolyn Greene

October 1998: A GROOM FOR GWEN (#3524)
by Jeanne Allan

December 1998: GABRIEL'S MISSION (#3532)
by Margaret Way

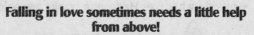

Falling in love sometimes needs a little help from above!

Available wherever Harlequin books are sold.

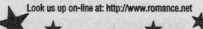

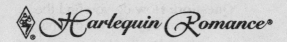
Harlequin Romance®

Get ready to meet the world's most eligible bachelors: they're sexy, successful and, best of all, they're all yours!

BACHELOR TERRITORY

Look out for these next two books:

September 1998:
WANTED: A PERFECT WIFE (#3521)
by Barbara McMahon

November 1998:
MY GIRL (#3529)
by Lucy Gordon

*There are two sides to every relationship—
and now it's his turn!*

Available wherever Harlequin books are sold.

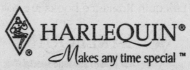
HARLEQUIN®
Makes any time special ™

Question: How do you find the
red-hot cowboy of your dreams?

Answer: Read on....

Texas Men Wanted! is a brand-new
miniseries in Harlequin Romance®.

Meet three very special heroines who are all looking for
very special Texas men—their future husbands! They've all
signed up with the Yellow Rose Matchmakers. The Yellow
Rose guarantees to find any woman her perfect partner....

So for the cutest cowboys in the whole state of Texas,
look out for:

HAND-PICKED HUSBAND
by Heather MacAllister in January 1999

BACHELOR AVAILABLE!
by Ruth Jean Dale in February 1999

THE NINE-DOLLAR DADDY
by Day Leclaire in March 1999

Available wherever
Harlequin Romance books are sold.

HARLEQUIN®
Makes any time special ™